Clint was surprised to see the men masked. He wore a with his white robes.

The room grew quiet as the men with guns came to attention. The Grand Master waved them off—for now . . .

"Mr. Adams, you're a brave man to come walking in here," the Master said, "but also a foolish one. Any one of these men would kill you. All I'd have to do is give the word."

"Then give it," Clint said, looking around the room, of which he had a panoramic view. He could see everyone. "These men know my reputation, right? Don't they, Al?"

"They know you're the Gunsmith all right," Al Fortune said.

"Then they know that I'll kill the first man who produces a gun," Clint said. He looked around the room, catching the eyes of as many men as he could. "Come on, who wants to die first for the Masons?"

DON'T MISS THESE
ALL-ACTION WESTERN SERIES
FROM THE BERKLEY PUBLISHING GROUP

THE GUNSMITH by J. R. Roberts
Clint Adams was a legend among lawmen, outlaws, and ladies. They called him . . . the Gunsmith.

LONGARM by Tabor Evans
The popular long-running series about Deputy U.S. Marshal Long—his life, his loves, his fight for justice.

SLOCUM by Jake Logan
Today's longest-running action Western. John Slocum rides a deadly trail of hot blood and cold steel.

BUSHWHACKERS by B. J. Lanagan
An action-packed series by the creators of Longarm! The rousing adventures of the most brutal gang of cutthroats ever assembled—Quantrill's Raiders.

DIAMONDBACK by Guy Brewer
Dex Yancey is Diamondback, a Southern gentleman turned con man when his brother cheats him out of the family fortune. Ladies love him. Gamblers hate him. But nobody pulls one over on Dex . . .

WILDGUN by Jack Hanson
The blazing adventures of mountain man Will Barlow—from the creators of Longarm!

TEXAS TRACKER by Tom Calhoun
Meet J.T. Law: the most relentless—and dangerous—manhunter in all Texas. Where sheriffs and posses fail, he's the best man to bring in the most vicious outlaws—for a price.

THE GUNSMITH

THE KNIGHTS OF MISERY

J. R. ROBERTS

JOVE BOOKS, NEW YORK

THE BERKLEY PUBLISHING GROUP
Published by the Penguin Group
Penguin Group (USA) Inc.
375 Hudson Street, New York, New York 10014, USA
Penguin Group (Canada), 90 Eglinton Avenue East, Suite 700, Toronto, Ontario M4P 2Y3, Canada
(a division of Pearson Penguin Canada Inc.)
Penguin Books Ltd., 80 Strand, London WC2R 0RL, England
Penguin Group Ireland, 25 St. Stephen's Green, Dublin 2, Ireland (a division of Penguin Books Ltd.)
Penguin Group (Australia), 250 Camberwell Road, Camberwell, Victoria 3124, Australia
(a division of Pearson Australia Group Pty. Ltd.)
Penguin Books India Pvt. Ltd., 11 Community Centre, Panchsheel Park, New Delhi—110 017, India
Penguin Group (NZ), 67 Apollo Drive, Rosedale, North Shore 0632, New Zealand
(a division of Pearson New Zealand Ltd.)
Penguin Books (South Africa) (Pty.) Ltd., 24 Sturdee Avenue, Rosebank, Johannesburg 2196,
South Africa

Penguin Books Ltd., Registered Offices: 80 Strand, London WC2R 0RL, England

This is a work of fiction. Names, characters, places, and incidents either are the product of the author's imagination or are used fictitiously, and any resemblance to actual persons, living or dead, business establishments, events, or locales is entirely coincidental.

THE KNIGHTS OF MISERY

A Jove Book / published by arrangement with the author

PRINTING HISTORY
Jove edition / November 2007

Copyright © 2007 by Robert J. Randisi.
Cover illustration by Sergio Giovine.

ISBN: 978-0-515-14369-0

JOVE®
Jove Books are published by The Berkley Publishing Group,
a division of Penguin Group (USA) Inc.,
375 Hudson Street, New York, New York 10014.
JOVE is a registered trademark of Penguin Group (USA) Inc.
The "J" design is a trademark belonging to Penguin Group (USA) Inc.

PRINTED IN THE UNITED STATES OF AMERICA

10 9 8 7 6 5 4 3 2 1

ONE

Roscoe Bookman eased himself carefully and quietly down the alley next to the Freemasons' temple of Utopia, Virginia. He could hear the voice coming from inside, so if he made any unnecessary noise they'd probably be able to hear him as well. On the other hand, they were pretty loud in there, so maybe it was safer for him to move a little more quickly and a little less quietly.

He came to the end of the alley and the back door of the building. He tried it and found it unlocked. When he opened it, the voice got even louder. He paused, trying to give his eyes time to adjust to the darkness inside. It was obvious that this door was giving him access to a room just behind their meeting room. As he closed the outer door behind him, he could see the light coming from beneath a connecting door. Whatever room he was in, it gave him an excellent vantage point from which to listen to their meeting, and maybe even get a look-see at what they were doing.

He moved to the connecting door and was able to make out what was being said. Someone was talking about Deputy Master Masons, and someone else mentioned the Grand Masters. Then someone said something about the Knights

1

of Masonry, which someone corrected—or changed—to the Knights of Misery.

Bookman wished he could write this stuff down, but he couldn't see well enough to put pencil to paper—both of which he happened to have in his pocket. He decided to take them out and try to write in the dark.

After a few attempts to write while still listening to the meeting, he remembered the lucifer matches in his pocket. He decided to take one out and strike it. He should only need a matter of seconds to make his notes. Switching the paper and pencil to one hand, he reached into his pocket, came out with one match, and struck it on his shoe to light it. The light given off by the flaring flame gleamed off the knife as it swooped forward and entered his stomach. He gasped from the shock, opening his hands and dropping both the pencil and paper as well as the match. As his attacker reversed the knife while it was still inside him and then brought it violently up, he heard his entrails splash onto the floor just seconds before he died. . . .

The man stepped through the door into the Masons' meeting hall and closed it quietly behind him. Another man was there, wearing a white robe.

"Is it done, brother?" he asked.

"It's done."

"Where is he?"

"Still in the back."

"Very well," the robed man said. "Wait until the meeting has adjourned and then dispose of it."

"Yes, brother."

"Remain where you are and don't let anyone enter the room."

"Yes, brother."

The robed man touched the other man on the arm and said, "You have done well."

"Thank you, brother."

The robed man removed his arm and went back to the meeting, unaware that some of Roscoe Bookman's blood had transferred from the killer's hand to the sleeve of his robe. His wife would discover the blood later and work hard to remove it.

Dan Flood waited until daybreak for Roscoe Bookman to return to the clearing they were using for their camp. When his partner did not return, he was faced with a quandary. Ride into town and look for him, or report back?

If Bookman had been killed, and Flood rode in and suffered the same fate, then none of what they had learned about the Masons in Utopia would be passed on.

As much as he wanted to go looking for his partner, he forced himself to break camp, saddle his horse, and head back to Washington to submit his report. Maybe Roscoe Bookman was alive, and Dan would be able to come back with help to rescue him; but if he was dead, Dan Flood had to make sure he hadn't died in vain.

TWO

Clint Adams's first view of Utopia, Virginia, made him think of rebirth. The sign stating the name of the town was obviously new. They could have just replaced the sign, but he knew it was more than that. The town had recently been renamed.

As he rode down the main street of Utopia, he could smell the newly cut wood that had been used to erect new buildings, and in a couple of places buildings were being constructed from brick. Utopia was definitely on the rise, which probably explained the name.

Clint knew that the word "utopia" was not necessarily a religious one, but on his way to the livery he passed three separate churches. However, they all appeared to have been in place for some time, and they also all looked to be in a state of disrepair. He wondered if they were poor, poorly tended, or simply abandoned.

He reached the livery and dismounted. There was no one in sight so he walked Eclipse, his big Darley Arabian, inside and shouted, "Hello! Anyone here?"

When no one answered, he dropped Eclipse's reins to the ground, knowing that the horse would not move from that spot, and moved deeper into the stable. There had to be an office somewhere, or perhaps someone out back.

Sure enough, when he found a back door and stepped through it, he saw a corral with two men in it. They seemed deep in conversation, although he couldn't imagine what about. There were no horses in the corral, just the two men. He did, however, see horses in some of the stalls inside, so he knew they were in business.

"Can I get some help?" he called out.

The two men turned to look at him. They were both in their forties, but just from their demeanor, and the looks on their faces, he could tell that one was superior to the other—if not by profession, then through some sort of class difference that showed in their clothes.

"Whataya need?" the better-dressed man asked.

"Just got to town," Clint responded, "want to put up my horse. This is the first place I saw."

"And the best," the man assured him. "Charlie here will take care of you, won't you, Charlie?"

"Sure, Mr. Wayne."

"And you'll remember what we talked about?"

"Yes, sir."

"Good, good." The man called Wayne looked at Clint. "Charlie'll take good care of your horse, mister. Welcome to town."

"Thanks," Clint said.

Wayne walked away while the man called Charlie watched him go, and then approached Clint.

"Problems?" Clint asked.

"Ain't we all got problems?" Charlie asked. "Where's your horse?"

"Inside."

"Let's go have a look."

Clint enjoyed the look on men's faces when they first

saw Eclipse. It had been the same with his previous horse, Duke. A look of surprise, respect, and awe.

"That's a mighty fine horse, mister."

"I know. Can you take care of him?"

"I'll take care of him before I touch any of these other nags," Charlie promised. "How long you gonna be in town?"

"I don't know," Clint said. "A few days at least."

"Well, it'll be my pleasure to look after this here animal," Charlie said, walking around Eclipse and examining him from all angles. "Yes, sir, I'll even give ya a good price."

"I don't care about the price," Clint said. "Just see that he's well looked after."

Charlie looked at Clint and said, "You got my word, mister."

Clint collected his saddlebags and rifle and then asked Charlie to recommend a hotel.

"We got a few that're real good," the liveryman said, "but the best is the Heritage."

"I think I passed that one when I came in."

"Nice rooms, baths, a real good dining room. You'll be real happy at the Heritage."

"Then that's where I'll be if you need me for anything."

"What did you say your business in town was?" Charlie asked.

"I didn't say," Clint said, and left.

The Heritage turned out to be the Heritage House, one of the newer buildings in town. As Clint entered, he saw a small but well-maintained lobby with new furniture, a brand-new oak front desk, and an attractive thirtyish woman behind it.

"Welcome to Heritage House," she said with a smile that transformed her from attractive to pretty.

"Thank you."

"I hope you're looking for a room," she said, "because if you aren't, you're in the wrong place."

"Then we're both in luck," he said, "because I'm looking for a room."

"Excellent." She spoke with an accent he knew was British. He'd been to England years ago, and loved the way the accent sounded on a pretty woman. "Just sign the register and I'll get your key."

He signed his name and wrote "Labyrinth, Texas" next to it. She handed him a key with a big smile, then reversed the book so she could read his name. He had gotten used to studying people when they heard or saw his name, and she did not show any sign of recognizing it.

"Well, Mr. Adams from Texas, welcome to Utopia."

"Thank you," he said. "It seems like a nice little town."

"We may be little," she said, "but we're growing."

"I can see that."

"And you'll like your room. It's clean."

"Glad to hear it."

"Please, let me know if you need anything, or if you're not happy. I'll do whatever I can to make your stay as pleasant as possible."

"Thank you . . ."

"Oh, I'm sorry," she said, "where are my manners? I'm Harriet Willis." She put her hand out. "I own the hotel."

"I'm impressed," he said, shaking her hand. "You own it, and work the desk?"

"My desk clerk was sick this morning," she said. "We all pitch in wherever we can."

"Does that mean that when your cook is sick you do the cooking too?" he asked.

She laughed and said, "I know you're joking, but there was a time when I did cook most of the meals. Luckily, I have two cooks now, so one is usually here. What I said about your room also goes for the dining room. If you're not happy, you let me know.' "

"So far, Harriet," he said, "I can't imagine why I wouldn't be."

THREE

Clint was not disappointed with the room. It was as clean as Harriet had promised. It also overlooked the main street, with no ledge on the outside of the window. That suited him. He was now in the habit of expecting someone to try to break into his room and kill him every night. When it didn't happen, he was happy, but he was always alert for it.

As he dropped his saddlebags on the bed and leaned his rifle against the wall in one corner, he realized he was very hungry. Because she had been right about the room, he was very hopeful about the condition of Harriet Willis's dining room. He decided he would eat first, then bathe later. Hopefully, no one else in the dining room would mind that he had just come off the trail.

He left the room and went downstairs.

After a fine meal in the dining room—one that had him stopping by the desk to compliment the owner—he left the hotel and went looking for a saloon. The bath had now been pushed to the next morning, replaced by a thirst for a cold beer.

He walked down the street, passed up two large saloons,

one on his side of the street and the other across the street. He kept walking until he came to a small saloon called Epiphany. It was an odd name and, as he entered, he saw that the inside lived up to it. No girls, no music, no gambling. He was starting to despair that they'd even have cold beer.

The place was about half full, and as he walked to the bar all eyes were on him, including the hostile eyes of the beefy, fiftyish bartender.

"Can I get a beer?" he asked.

"You're in the wrong place, friend," the barman said.

"For a beer?"

"For anything you want."

"Oh? Why's that?"

"You're a stranger."

"That's right," Clint said. "Just rode into town."

"We don't serve strangers," the man said. "There's plenty other saloons in town for you."

"Oh." Clint looked around. The other men in the place were still watching him. "This place is private?"

"Real private."

"Well, okay," Clint said. "It's your place. I guess you can serve whoever you want." He started to go, then turned back. "By the way, what's the name mean?"

The bartender gave him a hard stare and said, "It's just a name."

"Just a name," Clint said. "Okay, thanks, you've been real helpful."

All eyes continued to watch him until he was out the door.

Clint backtracked and chose one of the larger saloons. This one was called simply The Whiskey. He liked the name, and the sounds coming from it were more in keeping with his idea of a saloon—music, glasses clinking, loud voices.

However, when he entered and stopped just inside the door to take a look around, there was still no gambling going on.

This place was more like three-quarters full, which he found odd because there was still an hour or two to go before dusk. Did these people not have jobs to go to?

He walked up to the bar without fanfare, found himself a spot, and ordered a beer.

"Comin' up," the bartender said. As he set a mug down in front of Clint, he asked, "New in town?"

"Just got in today."

"Stayin' long?"

"I don't know. I'm not sure how friendly this town is."

"Whoa, friend," the man standing next to him said. "If you just got here, why would you say we ain't friendly?"

Clint told him how they wouldn't serve him in the first saloon he'd stopped in.

"Hell, that wasn't no saloon, that's a private club," the man said. "That was them—whataya call 'em—Masons?"

"Is that so?"

"Yep," the bartender said. "Gotta be a member to get a decent word from them fellers."

"Well, that explains it, I guess," Clint said. "At least you've been friendly, and the woman who runs the hotel was also."

"That'd be Harriet," the man said. "She's sweet as pie— and she don't only work there. She owns the Heritage House."

"I know, she told me."

"Ya got plans to stay in town awhile?"

"I'm just looking for a place to rest up before I continue on, so yeah, probably."

"Well, just make sure you stay away from them Masons, and you should find some real friendly people."

"I'll keep that in kind," Clint said, "but what is a Mason anyway?"

"I ain't exactly sure," the bartender said, "but around here they got themselves another name."

"And what's that?"

"Well," the man said, leaning in close, "they call themselves the Knights of Masonry. But folks hereabouts call 'em the Knights of Misery."

attention that the **Knights of Masonry**
   assassination."
of who?" Clint asked.
   Cleveland."

FOUR

The telegram had come to Clint in Labyrinth, Texas, a
month ago. The train had taken him to Washington, D.C.,
even faster than it ever had before. Clint couldn't believe
how fast train engines were going these days, and how
quickly a man could travel cross-country.

Once he arrived in Washington, he checked into a room
that had been reserved for him in a small hotel on K Street,
then walked two blocks to a small saloon where he met
with a man who went by the name Dutch.

Clint would have questioned having to meet with a man
who went by a single name, but this had all been in the
telegram—the hotel, and the saloon, and "Dutch." If the telegram had been from anyone but his friend Secret Service
Agent Jim West, he would have tossed it away and forgotten
about it. Clint entered, went to the bar, ordered a beer, and
walked to a table in the back. He had no idea what Dutch
looked like, so it would be up to the man to find him.

A few sets of eyes followed his progress to the table, curious locals who had never seen him there before. Clint
wondered why anyone would pick a local place like this for
a meeting, but the patrons soon lost interest and went back

to their conversations and their drinks. After ten minutes, as his beer was getting warm, a man walked in the front door wearing a heavy coat and a sour expression. He walked to the bar, greeted the bartender, who—to Clint's surprise—called him Dutch, and then ordered two beers. Armed with them, he walked to Clint's table and sat down, pushing the fresh beer across to him. He then opened his coat and sat back. He drank deeply from his beer, draining half and giving Clint a look at the shoulder rig he wore beneath the coat. Clint did not, however, think that this was the reason for opening the coat. It was just a byproduct of it.

"Mr. Adams," he said after he'd slaked his thirst, "my name is Dutch. Jim West told me to say hello to you for him."

"Do we shake hands?" Clint asked.

"No," Dutch said. "I'd prefer that we look like friends, not new acquaintances."

"Fine."

"I will remove my coat, though."

As Dutch stood and did that, Clint saw that he was a barrel-chested man in his mid-thirties, with a heavy mustache and large hands. Under the coat he wore a pin-striped jacket, which he kept on, probably to hide the gun.

"We're grateful that you made this trip," Dutch said, sitting back down.

"We?"

"You know," Dutch said, "we."

Clint was sure the man meant the Secret Service. He could have given him a hard time, but decided not to. Dutch did not look like the kind of man who had a sense of humor.

"I came because Jim West asked me to," Clint said.

"We understand that," Dutch said. "We also understand that you agreed to come and listen, not to accept whatever task we might ask you to undertake."

"I'd ne
Clint said.
"It's un
Clint pu
cold one.
"Mr. Ad
you?"
"They're
"That's
said. "The
have shared
ner working
have not bee
"Some f
they?" Clint
Dutch hel
tracks.
"That's re
"I assume
chose it."
"It is safe
but that does
room."
Now Clint
a Freemason
"Mr. Adan
in Virginia wl
"Why cal
Clint asked.
"Apparentl
Freemasonry.
"And that's
Now Dutc
share a secret.

"It's come to ou
might be planning a
"An assassinatio
"President Grov

FIVE

Clint had never heard them called the Knights of Misery until he actually came to town.

"Where does that name come from?" he asked the bartender.

"That's what they bring to folks around here who aren't members of their group," the man said. "Misery."

"I thought they were supposed to be a religious group," Clint said, as if ignorant of what Masons actually were. He had, in fact, been ignorant before he went to Washington and spoke with Dutch.

Of course, Dutch and the government were not concerned with whether or not the Masons were religious. It was whether they were murderers. . . .

"We sent two men in undercover to see what was going on," Dutch had told Clint that evening in the Washington, D.C., saloon.

"What did they find out?"

"Only one came back," Dutch said, "and what he knew was inconclusive."

"What happened to the other man?"

"We don't know, and neither did his partner," Dutch said. "He just disappeared."

"Dead?"

"We assume."

"From what the first man told you, do you think they would actually kill him?"

"Our man witnessed many forms of violence at the hands of these Masons," Dutch said, "but he never saw them kill anyone."

"So you don't know—"

"What we know is that they're dangerous," Dutch said. "They've gone way beyond Freemasonry into violence and intimidation."

"So what do you want me to do about it?"

"We need somebody else to go in," Dutch said. "Somebody smart, tough, competent enough to get in and out alive, and someone who is not a member of a government organization."

Clint leaned back.

"You think you have an informant in your midst," he said.

Dutch sat back.

"We don't know how else they identified our man."

"One of your men," Clint said. "Have you wondered about that? How they identified only one?"

"We have wondered," he said, "and we wanted to ask his partner about it."

"And?"

"Since he returned to Washington, we've talked with him once."

"So why not again?"

"Because since his return, he has also disappeared," Dutch said. "Before you ask, we don't know if it was willingly or not."

Clint picked up his beer and sipped it.

"So you want me to just ride into town—what town is it?"

"Utopia," Dutch said, "Utopia, Virginia. Ever heard of it?"

"No."

"That's because up to a year ago it was called something else—a town nobody had ever heard of before. The Masons changed the name to Utopia."

"Doesn't that mean . . . a happy place?"

"Also a nonexistent place," Dutch said. "A fantasy place."

"Doesn't sound like any of those things to me," Clint said. "What brought your attention to it?"

"An ex-mayor named Harold Feeley," Dutch said. "He got in touch with us just before the town was renamed and he was replaced with a mayor who is a Freemason."

"And where is the ex-mayor now—wait, don't tell me. He's disappeared."

"Right."

Clint thought a moment.

"Well, these people can't all just be disappearing," he said finally. "Somebody's got to be dead."

"And we need somebody to go in there and find out for sure," Dutch said.

"And if I do?"

"Then we'll go in there with federal marshals and clean it out."

"Why not go in now?"

"We need proof," Dutch said. "That's the law."

"Who's the head of the Secret Service right now?" Clint asked.

"Hamilton Caine took over two years ago," Dutch said. "He has a military background, still holds the rank of general."

Allan Pinkerton started the Secret Service during the Civil War. Several men had succeeded him since he left to concentrate on his detective agency. Clint had met several whom he did not get along with, but whenever he did work for the Secret Service, it was always at the behest of his friend Jim West.

"I've never worked with him," Clint said. "I didn't get along very well with some of the other heads of the Service."

"He's . . . different," Dutch said. "You'd get along with him."

"Well," Clint said, "I don't really have to in order to do this job, do I?"

"Probably not."

They sat in silence for a few moments, during which time they finished their beers.

"Will you do it?" Dutch finally asked.

"Get me another cold beer and I'll tell you my decision," Clint said.

The man nodded, stood up, and strode to the bar. By the time he returned with two cold beers, Clint told him he'd do it.

SIX

Clint left the saloon and went back to his hotel, knowing more about the Freemasons—or the Knights of Misery—than he did when he first rode into Utopia.

Harriet Willis was behind the desk when he walked in. When she saw him, she smiled widely.

"Takin' in some of our town?" she asked.

"A little," he admitted. "Didn't get a very friendly welcome in one of the saloons, though."

"You went into the Knights of Misery place, didn't you?"

"I did," he said. "Guess I won't make that mistake twice."

"They're terrible people," she said.

"Did I hear somebody say that one of them was the mayor?"

"You did," she said, "and he's the worst of them."

"Seems to me the town is growing," Clint said.

"That doesn't mean it's getting any better," she said. "The Knights do what they do for their own benefit, and nobody else's."

"You sound like you know them well."

"I know some of them, yes," she said. "And they're not all bad. It's just. . . ." She trailed off.

"What?"

She shook her head.

"I shouldn't be talking about it to a stranger," she said.

Clint thought about pushing it, then decided not to. He'd score more points now by letting it go.

"All right, Harriet," he said. "I don't want you to say anything you're not comfortable saying. I'll just go to my room."

"I hope I haven't offended you," she said quickly as he made for the stairs.

"Not at all," he said. "Don't worry about it."

"You're not turning in, are you?" she asked. "This early? We have some very good saloons in town . . . or so I'm told."

"Not tonight," he said. "I've got a Mark Twain I'm reading, and I traveled a long way today."

"I enjoy Mark Twain as well."

He smiled and said, "Okay," and went to his room.

He figured she'd be anxious to talk tomorrow.

Clint read for several hours before he was tired enough to go to sleep. He woke in the morning refreshed, and hungry. He felt he'd made some progress the short time he was in town, but he certainly didn't have anything he could send back to Washington. He figured today he'd have a talk with the local lawman, but first he had to find out if he too was a Mason—or a Knight. That meant reaping the seeds he'd planted the night before with Harriet Willis.

He washed, dressed, strapped on his gun, and went down to the lobby, expecting to once again find Harriet behind the desk. Instead, there was a young man there— a young man with a long neck and a ready smile.

"Good morning, sir," he greeted. "You must be Mr. Adams."

"How did you know that?"

"We only had one new guest yesterday," he said, "and you are the only guest I don't recognize."

"You know all the guests on sight and by name?"

"Oh, yes, sir," the young man said. "We pride ourselves here on service. I have to know who the guests are in order to serve them better."

"That's an admirable attitude," Clint said.

"Thank you."

"What's your name?"

"Frederick, sir. Frederick Anderson."

"Frederick," Clint said. "Can I call you Fred?"

"If you wish."

"Freddy?"

"Please don't."

"Fred then," Clint said. "Can you tell me where your boss is?"

"I'm not sure I know, Mr. Adams," Fred said. "She had to work my shift yesterday, so I'll bet she's sleeping late this morning. Is there something I can help you with?"

"Well, she and I were having a discussion about the Freemasons," Clint said.

"Really?"

"Yes," Clint said. "She was sort of filling me in on what's going on here in town."

"That's not something we usually talk about," Fred said warily.

"Oh, I understand that," Clint said. "In fact, she became a bit uncomfortable, so I broke off the discussion and went to my room."

"I see."

"But since you and I are men," Clint said, "I thought you might fill me in a bit more."

"Well . . ."

"Unless you're afraid," Clint said. "I can understand if you're too scared to tell—"

"Well, it ain't that, sir," Fred said. "I ain't afraid, you understand."

"Oh, I understand."

"It's just . . . frowned on, you know, to be talkin' about them."

"Well," Clint said, "Miss Willis—it is Miss, isn't it?"

"Yes, sir."

"Miss Willis mentioned to me that the mayor was a Mason," Clint said. "Now, I was just wondering if, when he took over as mayor, he replaced other, uh, civil servants. Like, say, the sheriff."

Fred looked around the empty lobby, then leaned in. Clint leaned in as well.

"Well, sir," he said, "it's generally known that the new mayor would like to replace the sheriff, but the sheriff was elected."

"Seems to me if a mayor wanted to push out a sheriff he could," Clint said. "Couldn't he just fire him?"

"Not without just cause."

"So how much longer till the next election for sheriff?"

"About a year."

"Do you think the two of them can get along for a year?"

"Just between you and me, sir . . ."

"Oh, I won't tell anyone," Clint promised him. "I swear."

"I don't think the mayor and the sheriff could get along for a minute."

"Well," Clint said, "that's real helpful, Fred. Thank you."

"You're welcome, sir." The boy leaned back. "Is there anything else I can do for you?"

"No," Clint said, "you've helped me just fine. I'm going to go have breakfast now."

"Would you like me to recommend a place?" Fred asked eagerly.

Clint started to say no, then thought, why not?

"Sure, Fred, why don't you do that?"

SEVEN

Clint left the small café Fred had sent him to, determined never to take the kid's word for a restaurant again. His eggs had been runny and his steak tough and—biggest sin of all—the coffee had been weak.

But his belly was full, which had been the point. From the café, he went directly to the sheriff's office. He thought the best way to play this was to announce his presence to the lawman, so nobody thought he was trying to sneak into town. He knew that once he'd signed the register in the hotel, the word would get around.

He entered the lawman's office, found it empty. He checked the cell block, but there was no one in there. As he turned to leave, the front door opened and a man wearing a badge came in. The two men startled each other, and then laughed about it.

"Sorry," the lawman said, "didn't expect to see anyone in here. I'm Sheriff Gentile. What can I do for you?"

The sheriff was in his forties, had probably been wearing a badge for some time. He had the look of an old lawman.

"Sheriff, I just wanted to let you know that I came into

26

town yesterday. I'm registered at that hotel run by Miss Willis."

"Well, that's nice to know," the sheriff said, "but why are you tellin' me this?"

"My name's Clint Adams."

The man had started to walk to his desk, and stopped in his tracks. He turned and faced Clint, his face showing that he was all business.

"What's the Gunsmith want in Utopia?" he asked.

"Well, for one thing," Clint said, "I'm wondering why I'm in a town called Utopia. Wasn't this called something else, say, as late as last year?"

The sheriff's distaste showed on his face as he said, "Yeah, we used to be called Beldon, but the new mayor came in and changed the town's name."

"Just like that?" Clint asked. "Can he do that?"

"Well, he took it to the town council, but they all backed him because they're all . . ." He stopped short, maybe because he thought he was giving away too much information.

"Masons?" Clint finished for him.

"Yeah," the sheriff said, "that's what I was gonna say. How'd you know?"

"Well, I've only been here since yesterday, but I've already heard about Freemasons and Knights of Misery," Clint explained.

"Folks around here got big mouths," Gentile said.

"Well, I did happen to walk into the wrong saloon, and they weren't very friendly."

"Ah," Gentile said, "now I understand."

He turned, walked to his desk, and sat down.

"How long you plannin' on stayin' around?" he asked Clint.

"I don't know," Clint said. "I'm just passing through. Usually, if I find a town friendly I'll stay awhile, but this one sort of confuses me. I mean, the bartender in the saloon last night was friendly enough, and the folks over at the hotel—"

"Mr. Adams, most folks are friendly around here," Gentile said. "The few you find who ain't will be Freemasons, and that's a shame."

"Masons, or Knights of Misery?" Clint asked.

"I don't know much about the Masons," Gentile said. "Me, I thought they was religious. But this bunch . . . these Knights, as they call themselves. They're just plain mean."

"I heard something about you and the mayor maybe not getting along."

"You heard right," Gentile said. "He's right in the middle of that whole mess. Look, why don't you have a seat?"

"Mess?" Clint asked, sitting down across from the lawman.

"I mean the Masons," Gentile said. "Knights, whatever they wanna call themselves."

"They give you any trouble?"

"I ain't never had any of them in my jail, if that's what you're askin'."

"So they haven't broken any laws?"

"I'm sure they have," Gentile said. "I just can't never get nobody to point a finger at them."

"Too scared, you mean?" Clint asked. "Intimidated?"

"I suppose," Gentile said. "Hey, why are you so interested?"

"I'm a curious gent," Clint said. "It's my one and only flaw."

"Only flaw?" The lawman was obviously referring to his reputation.

"Well, as I see it," Clint said.

"Well, look, Mr. Adams," Gentile said. "I appreciate you comin' by to announce your presence in town. And I'm sure you're gonna do your best to stay out of trouble."

"I always try to stay out of trouble, Sheriff."

"Well, good," the lawman said. "Stay in town as long as you like. I'm sure you'll run into friendly folks. Miss Willis is good people. She'll treat you right over there at her place. And we got some good saloons in town."

"That's what Miss Willis was telling me she'd, uh, heard."

"Well, she's right." Gentile hitched himself up in his chair, put his hands on his desk. "Is there anything else I can do for you?"

"No," Clint said, "I guess I've taken up enough of your time."

He stood up, headed for the door.

"Oh, one more question," Clint said. "I haven't seen any deputies around town."

"I got two," Gentile said. "They know to stay away from me during the day. They make rounds at night."

"Masons?"

Sourly, Gentile said, "Yeah, both of them."

"Fire them."

"Can't," Gentile said. "Both of them are the mayor's nephews."

EIGHT

Mayor Benjamin Calhoun looked up as the door to his office opened.

"Mayor, somebody out here to see you," his secretary said.

"Do I want to see them, Esther?"

"He says he has some information for you."

"Well, then, send him in."

"Yes, sir."

She still called him sir, even though he'd had her up on his desk more than once. In her thirties, she was lusty, single, and knew that the mayor and his wife had separate bedrooms. He also thought she enjoyed being with him because of the power he wielded in town. Except for one other man, he was the most powerful person in town—and he intended to see that change.

The door opened and Esther ushered a young man into his office.

"What's on your mind, son?"

"I thought you'd be interested in knowing who had just come to town, Mayor."

"Is that a fact?" the mayor asked. "And what were you expecting in return for this information?"

The young man looked confused.

"Nothin', sir," he said. "I was just hopin' to be helpful to the Knights."

"Well, that's admirable, boy," the Mayor said, "real admirable. Have a seat."

The young man sat down.

"Comfortable?"

"Yes, sir."

"Then tell me your news."

"Clint Adams came to town yesterday," the young man said. "He's stayin' over at the hotel."

"Clint Adams."

"Yes, sir."

"The Gunsmith?"

"Yes, sir."

"That is interesting," the mayor admitted. "Did he give any indication of how long he'd be staying?"

"No, sir," the young man said, "but he did say he had gone into the Knights' saloon and was rather, uh, rudely greeted."

The mayor sat back in his chair.

"I did hear something about a stranger wandering in there."

The young man didn't know what to say to that, so he sat quietly and waited.

"I tell you what," the mayor said. "Keep an eye on him for me, report his movements, or anything you might hear him say. I'll check around town and see who else he might have talked to."

"I know he's talked to Miss Willis."

The mayor frowned.

"That woman," he said, shaking his head. "You'll have to find out what she's told him."

"Yes, sir."

The mayor leaned forward again.

"It's a very good thing you came in with this information," Mayor Calhoun said. "It's not something I'll forget."

"Thank you, sir," the young man said. "That's all I ask. I—I'd like to join the Knights one day soon."

"I'll keep that in mind," the mayor said.

The young man sat there a few moments before he realized the mayor was done with him.

"Well, I better get back," he said, getting to his feet.

"You do that," the mayor said. "And send my girl in when you leave."

"Yes, sir."

Calhoun sat back in his chair, folded his hands across his belly, which stretched the buttons of his vest.

When Esther entered, he said, "Close the door behind you."

She did.

"Lock it."

Now she knew why he wanted her. She locked the door, walked to his desk, already unbuttoning her dress. He watched as she peeled it down, revealing full, firm breasts with swollen brown nipples. She dropped the dress to the floor and stepped away, then did a turn the way she knew he liked so he could see her chubby buttocks.

He pushed his chair away from his desk so she could get down on her knees in front of him. She opened his pants and pulled out his erect penis, began to roll it in her hands, against her cheek, between her breasts, and finally took it into her mouth. Even when Calhoun and his wife were on good terms, she'd never do anything like this.

He held her head with one hand as it bobbed up and down on him, slid the other hand between them to pinch her nipples. He didn't have time to spread her out on the desk and have her, so he let her finish him this way, then told her to get up and get dressed. She pouted, but obeyed. He didn't fool himself. Ben Calhoun was nothing if not a realist. He knew a beautiful woman like Esther could have anyone she wanted. Why would she want a potbellied, middle-aged man like him? Because of the power he wielded, that's why.

"Esther, find Al Fortune and get him up here," he told her.

"Yes, sir."

"Send my wife a message. Tell her to have supper without me. I'll eat at the club."

"Yes, sir."

"That's all."

She straightened herself out, then walked to the door, unlocked it, and opened it.

"Oh, before you go."

"Yes?"

"Remind me of the name of that young man who was just in here."

"That was Frederick Anderson, Mr. Mayor."

As she left, he was writing the name down.

NINE

Clint felt that he had initiated all the contact he could. Now he had to sit back, wait, and see if his presence in town was of any interest to the Knights of Misery. He didn't want to push and make them suspicious of him. They had to believe that he was just passing through, and he'd told enough people that.

As he approached his hotel, he saw the clerk, Fred, going in the front door. When he entered, Fred and Harriet Willis were standing behind the desk, and she was apparently unhappy about something.

"—can't just walk away from the desk," she was saying. "What if a guest needed something? Or someone had to check in?"

"I'm sorry," he said. "I, uh, I had to go out and do somethin'. I wasn't gone long."

"Frederick, if you do something like this again, I'm gonna have to let you go."

"No, no," the young man pleaded, "you can't. I'll—I'll never do it again, I promise."

At that moment, Harriet noticed Clint coming through the front door.

"We'll finish talking about this later," she said. "For now, just go back to work."

"Yes, ma'am."

She came around from behind the desk to greet Clint. She was wearing jeans and boots and a man's shirt. She touched her hair as he approached.

"Is there a problem?" he asked.

"Oh, no, not really," she said. "You just have to stay on top of your employees sometimes."

"He seems like a dependable lad."

"Usually, he is," she said, shaking her head. "It's not like him to walk away from the desk without so much as a by-your-leave."

"Maybe he had an emergency."

"What have you been doing today?" she asked.

"Just walking around," he said. "Getting acquainted with some of the people."

"Oh? Like who?"

"Well, the sheriff for one."

"Really?" she asked. "What business would you have with the sheriff your second day in town?"

"It's just something I like to do, look in on the local law when I ride into a town."

"Oh, because of your . . . reputation?"

"Yes, that's exactly the reason," he said. "When I checked in, you never let on that you knew who I was."

"To tell you the truth, I didn't realize it at first," she admitted. "It wasn't until later, when I looked at your name again, that it came to me." She rubbed her arms, a gesture he found attractive at that moment. "I don't mind telling you I found it thrilling to have you registered in my hotel."

Clint was sure that, being a woman, if it thrilled her that much, she must have told some of her friends.

"I don't know how thrilling it is," he said. "I'm really just like any other man."

"Do you really believe that?"

"I'd like to," he said after a moment. "Fact is, folks won't really let me."

"Well, I'm sorry if I added to that," she said. "I've just never really met somebody . . . uh . . . a man like . . . a famous person."

"That's all right, Harriet," he said. "I wouldn't let it worry you."

"I—I just wouldn't want to do anything to offend you."

"Believe me, Harriet," he said, "you haven't offended me."

"Good, I—"

"But it will offend me if you don't accept my invitation to supper tonight."

"Oh . . . supper . . . well, I—"

"Just tell me what time you're available," he said. "I'll come by your home, or we can meet here."

"Well, since this is my home," she said, "I suppose we can meet here. I—I have a room downstairs."

"Good," he said. "Then I'll pick you up here at . . . say, five o'clock?"

"Five would be good," she said. "I—I'll have to get back here by seven."

"Okay then," he said. "I'll see you at five."

"All right," she said. "Thank you."

Clint headed for the stairs, noticed that young Frederick had been listening intently to his conversation with Harriet. Could it be the young man was a little jealous? Or did his interest have to do with something else entirely?

TEN

"Al Fortune is here," Esther said, sticking her head into the mayor's office.

"Send him on in, sweetheart, send him on in," Calhoun said.

Calhoun stood up as Al Fortune entered. Fortune was a tall, almost cadaverously thin man in his thirties. Put a dark suit and stovepipe hat on him, and he'd look like an undertaker. He was clad in worn trail clothes, and while the leather of his gun belt was cracked, Calhoun knew that the gun resting there was in perfect working order.

"Al, good to see you," Calhoun said, shaking hands with the man he kept on the payroll for both delicate and dangerous jobs. This one had all the makings of both.

"Drink?" Calhoun asked.

"Not if all you got is that piss water you drink," Fortune said.

"Napoleon brandy?"

"I'll pass," Fortune said, dropping himself into a chair.

"Uh, yes, all right." Calhoun walked around behind his desk and sat.

"You got a job for me?" Fortune asked.

37

"I've got something I'd like you to do, yes," the mayor said. "It's just come to my attention that a man named Clint Adams is in town."

Fortune sat up a bit straighter.

"I heard that too," he said, "but I didn't believe it."

"Well, it's true," Calhoun said.

"You want me to kill 'im?"

"Do you think you could?"

Fortune rubbed his hand over the gray-black stubble on his chin.

"I'd sure like ta try," he said thoughtfully. "I mean, if you just want 'im, I could do that from a rooftop. Ya know, shoot 'im in the back? But I'd sure rather try him from the front."

"Well," Calhoun said, "as of now I've really got no reason to want him dead. I would, however, like to find out what he's doing here."

"And you want me ta ask 'im?"

"I want you to engage him."

"What?"

"Meet him," Calhoun said, "talk to him, make friends if you have to, but find out what he's doing in town."

"Make friends?"

"Yes, I know it's not something you usually do, but it seems to me you're the man in town who would be most like him. Am I wrong?"

"I dunno," Fortune said. "All we know about him is his rep."

"A man with a gun," Calhoun said. "That description fits you as well, doesn't it?"

"It fits me, all right," Fortune said, "but I suppose we'll have to find out for sure if it fits him or not."

"Well," Calhoun said, "let's just start with meeting him."

Fortune thought it over a few moments, then said, "I want double my usual fee."

"What?"

"This is the Gunsmith we're talkin' about."

"I only want you to talk to him."

"That's why I'm only askin' for double," Fortune said. "If you want me to kill him, I'm gonna ask for . . . uh, more than triple."

"Quadruple?"

Fortune grinned.

"That's it."

Calhoun hesitated, then said, "What if I told you this was a task for the Knights?"

"What do I care about the Knights?" Fortune asked. "I work for you, Mayor, not them. I don't believe in no religion."

"The Knights are not only about religion, Al," Calhoun said. "That's only part of it."

"Well, it ain't a part I'm interested in," Fortune said. "My religion is money. If you don't wanna pay, why don't you get somebody from inside the Knights to do this for you?"

"We don't have anybody like that."

"Then I guess you're stuck with me," Fortune said. "You still want me ta do this?"

"I still want you to."

"For double?"

"Yes," Calhoun said, "double." He could take the money from the town treasury, and not his own pocket.

"Okay then," Fortune said, standing up. "Where's he stayin'?"

"He's at that little hotel owned by that Willis woman."

"Harriet?" Fortune smiled. "Well, this job may be more pleasant than I thought."

"I'm paying you to do a job, Al," Calhoun said, "not chase some woman's skirts."

"Don't worry, Mayor," Fortune said. "I'm a real talented fella. I can do both."

ELEVEN

Clint didn't stay in his room for long. There was nothing to be accomplished there. He put the Twain book aside and went downstairs to the lobby. Frederick was manning the desk. When he saw Clint, he suddenly looked nervous, totally unlike the friendly young man he'd been that morning. As Clint started toward the desk, Frederick suddenly ducked his head.

"Hey, Fred," Clint said.

The young man jerked his head up.

"Yes, sir?"

"Everything all right?"

"Um, everything is fine, sir," Fred said. "I'm just, uh, busy."

"Seems like I walked in on something earlier," Clint said, "between you and your boss."

"Oh, that," Frederick said. "I just, uh, did something stupid. She was right to yell at me. I'll never do it again."

"Well, I guess that's good then."

"Yes," Frederick said, "we get along just fine, me and Miss Willis."

"Could it be you have a little crush on her?"

41

Frederick's eyes widened.

"Miss Willis?" he said. "Oh, no, she's . . . old."

"Old, huh?"

"She must be at least . . . thirty."

"How old are you, Fred?"

"I'm twenty, sir."

"Yeah, you're right," Clint said. "Thirty is pretty old."

"Yes, sir."

"I'll see you later, Fred."

"Yes, sir."

Maybe the young man didn't have a crush on his boss, but something was going on with him. It wasn't Clint's job to solve his problem, though.

Clint went back to The Whiskey, the saloon he'd stopped into yesterday.

"Hey," the bartender said when Clint stopped at the bar, "still here, huh?"

"Still here."

"Beer?"

"Yes."

The barman placed a frothy beer in front of Clint and then leaned on the bar.

"How are things goin' with Harriet?"

"I've got a very nice room," Clint said. "Hey, maybe you can help me with something."

"What's that?"

"She's got a young fellow working for her, named Frederick."

"That'd be Freddy Anderson."

"I thought he didn't like being called Freddy."

The man smiled.

"That's kinda why I do it," he said. "He's kind of a serious kid, doesn't take ribbin' too well."

"So that's why you do it."

"Exactly."

"Well, what else can you tell me about him other than he's serious and has no sense of humor?"

"That's about it," the bartender said. "Why?"

"Well, he was real friendly when I came down this morning, but this afternoon he seemed a little bit skittish."

"Maybe he realized who you were."

That might explain it. After all, it had taken Harriet a little while to place him.

"I guess that could be it."

"You're probably used to makin' folk nervous, ain't ya?"

"That's not something you get used to . . . What's your name?"

"Oh, my name's Cook, Bud Cook." Bud stuck his hand out and Clint shook it.

"Been in this town long?"

"Too long," Bud said. "If I could find a buyer for this place, I'd be outta here."

"Any particular reason?"

"Yeah, one," Bud said. "The one we were talkin' about yesterday."

"The Masons?"

"Or the Knights, whatever they wanna be called. They're gonna take over the whole town soon. I don't really want to be around to be part of that."

Bud excused himself to serve somebody else down the line. Clint grabbed his beer, turned his back to the bar, and surveyed the room. It was just about that time that a tall, painfully thin man came through the batwing doors and headed for the bar.

TWELVE

Al Fortune had gone to the hotel first and spoken with the clerk, Fred Anderson. From the young man he got Clint's description, so that as soon as he entered The Whiskey—the third saloon he'd tried—he recognized Clint standing at the bar.

Fortune was not very adept at making friends. In fact, he didn't care if he never had a friend in the world. So he wasn't at all sure how to approach Clint Adams. Luckily, he knew the bartender by name, so that gave him a way to go. He walked to the bar, stood a few feet away from the Gunsmith, and asked the bartender for a beer.

"Comin' up," Bud Cook said.

When the barman brought his beer, Fortune said, "Thanks, Bud. Anythin' new goin' on?"

"In here, Al?" Cook said. "What's gonna be new in here?"

"Just makin' small talk," Fortune said, which sounded false even to his own ears. He decided to just take the bull by the horns. He looked over at Clint and asked, "New in town?"

Clint looked over at him.

"That's right. Rode in yesterday."

"And you're still here?" Fortune asked. He laughed, felt he'd made contact. "What is there to keep you here?"

"Actually," Clint said, turning toward Fortune, "I was just looking for a place to rest for a few days."

"Well, then, you found the right place," Fortune said. "Ain't much ta do around here but rest."

"How long have you been here?"

"Believe me, I been here too long."

Fortune had no way of knowing that was the second time someone had said that to Clint.

"I work around here," Fortune said then. "But I been thinking about hittin' the trail."

"Oh? What do you do?"

"Odd jobs," Fortune said. "This and that. I'm kind of a handyman."

Fortune knew how he looked. In fact, he cultivated the look. His clothes were not clean or new, he'd had the same gun belt for years, and nobody would ever take him for a man who made his way with a gun.

Handyman seemed a good way to go.

Clint doubted that this fellow was a handyman of any sort. In fact, the way he wore his gun indicated to Clint that that was what he was handy with. He didn't dress well, and he needed a new gun belt, but the gun itself seemed well cared for, and he wore it low where he'd be able to snatch it quick with his long arms.

"You mind if I ask you a few questions?" said Clint.

"About what?"

Clint moved a little closer, so their conversation wouldn't be too loud.

"I'm curious about some things I've been hearing since I got to town."

The man frowned.

"My name's Clint," Clint said.

"Al."

The two men did not shake hands. Neither wanted their gun hand to be that occupied, another indication to Clint about what the man did for a living.

"Al, what do you know about the Masons in town who call themselves the Knights of Misery?"

"I know enough to steer clear of them."

"So you're not a member?"

"Hell, no."

"You mind if I ask why not?"

"Well, Clint, to tell you the truth, I'm not much of a joiner—but even if I was, the Knights are not the kind of group I'd wanna join."

"Too religious?"

"You know, they tell me that they're not all that religious," Al said. "And if they're not a religious group, then I'm confused."

"I hear they do things that aren't so religious."

"Do things?"

"Yes. They sound to me more like a gang than a . . . a . . ." Clint groped for the words. "I don't even know what the Masons call themselves."

"I think they say they're a fraternal organization," Al said. "I mean, I hear them callin' each other brother, ya know? And I don't need no brothers."

The man sounded like he didn't want any brothers, or friends. So, Clint wondered, why was he being so accessible?

"You want another beer?" Clint asked.

Al looked at his half-full glass, drained it quickly, and said, "Why not?"

THIRTEEN

It was entirely possible that this fella Al had heard that Clint was in town and had decided to feel him out, with an eye toward trying his luck. Why else would a man like him even start up a conversation with a stranger?

Over a second beer, they discussed the good and bad points of the town of Utopia, and one of the bad points Al mentioned was the name.

"I never heard such a stupid name for a town," he said. "What the hell does it even mean?"

"You got me," Clint said, playing dumb.

"Hey, Bud?" Al called.

"Yep?"

"You know what Utopia means?"

Bud rubbed his chin.

"I thought it had somethin' to do with Heaven myself," the bartender said.

"Heaven," Al said. He looked at Clint. "There's somethin' else I don't believe in, another reason for me to stay away from anything that has to do with religion."

"That brings up a question," Clint said.

"What?" Al asked, and Bud leaned in close to hear.

"Churches," Clint said. "I haven't seen any churches in town."

"We used ta have three churches, didn't we, Bud?" Al asked the bartender.

"Yeah, we did," Bud said, "but the Knights closed 'em down."

"So where do people go on Sunday?" Clint asked.

"Well," Bud said, "this never was much of a church-goin' town, so I guess folks don't miss 'em so much."

"Do the Masons—uh, the Knights—have any kind of Sunday ceremony?"

"Not that I know of," Bud said. "They might, for their members."

"Bud's like me," Al said. "Don't want nothin' ta do with them Knights."

"Not so loud," Bud said, looking around. "You never know when you're standin' next to one of them."

"He's right," Al said, "anybody in the room could be a Knight."

"So who's the leader of the Knights?" Clint asked. "The mayor?"

"The mayor?" Bud asked before Al could say a word. "If he is, I hope he runs them better than he runs the town."

"He's not much of a mayor?" Clint asked.

"He don't do nothin' but sit in his office," Bud said. "This town was growin' before he took over. Now we've come to a complete stop."

"I heard he was a member of the Knights," Clint said, looking at Al.

"Might be," Al said. "I don't pay much attention to what them Knights do. I just try ta stay away from them."

"Seems to me a lot of the merchants in town would be mad if the progress just stopped."

"They are," Bud said.

"Why don't they do something?"

"Like what?" Bud asked.

"Toss the mayor out on his ear, for one."

"Don't nobody in town want to try that," the bartender said. "The Knights put him in office. I'm sure they'll do whatever they have to do to keep him there."

Al was drinking his beer while Bud was talking, and now placed the empty mug down on the bar.

"Another one, Al?" Bud asked.

"Sure," Al said, "and give one to my friend Clint here."

Bud paused. He'd never heard Al Fortune refer to anyone as his "friend." He wondered idly if Al even knew Clint's last name.

"Mr. Adams?" he said deliberately.

Clint looked at the barman, understood what he'd just done, and wondered himself about what would happen.

"Sure," he said. "I'll take another."

As Bud went for the beers, Al said, "Adams, huh?"

"That's right," Clint said, "but you knew that already, didn't you?"

Al stared at him, then said, "I'd heard you was in town. I didn't believe it, but when you told me your first name I had an idea."

"And what would your last name be?"

"Me? I'm Al Fortune, but that wouldn't mean anythin' ta you. It don't mean nothin' to anybody in this town."

Bud brought the two fresh beers and set them down, then moved away. He thought it would be better if he wasn't involved in their conversation anymore.

He knew Al Fortune had something in mind because he hadn't once mentioned to Clint Adams that he worked for the mayor.

Bud knew that was something the Gunsmith would have found interesting.

FOURTEEN

"Al." Mayor Calhoun was surprised to find Al Fortune standing on his doorstep.

"I went to your office and found it locked," Fortune said. "Figured you went home."

"What can I do for you?"

"I saw Adams," Fortune said. "Do you want to talk about it on your doorstep?"

"No, no, of course not," the mayor said. "Come on in. I was just sitting down to supper."

Fortune did not expect an invitation, and he didn't get one. He was good enough to work for the mayor, but not to eat with him. That didn't bother him, though. He was only interested in money. He could buy his own food.

"My wife is upstairs," the mayor said as they arrived in his living room. "Can I get you a drink?"

Fortune gave the mayor a look.

"Oh, right," Calhoun said, "you don't like what I drink. Well, what do you have for me then?"

"I found Adams at The Whiskey," Fortune said. "We talked over some beers."

Calhoun could tell that because he could smell the beer on Fortune.

"And what did you come up with?"

"He's just passing through."

"That's it?"

Fortune shrugged.

"That's what he said," Fortune responded. "He travels around the country, sometimes aimlessly. He stops in towns when he get tired, looks for a place to rest. That's what this is. A rest stop."

"And you believed him?" the mayor asked.

Fortune shrugged.

"We were just two fellas drinkin' beers," he said. "Why would he lie?"

"Al," Calhoun said, "I have somebody to answer to, you know. I have to see the Grand Master tonight. I need to have something to tell him."

"Tell him Clint Adams is just passin' through," Fortune said. *Then,* he thought, *tell him to teach you to drink real liquor.*

"You expect me to pay you for this information?" the mayor asked.

"Do you want to go and ask the Gunsmith himself what he's doin' in town?" Fortune asked. "And then call him a liar when he tells you?"

Calhoun stared at Fortune, then looked away.

"I'll have my money now, Mayor."

"Are you still willing to take a run at Adams if . . . if the need arises?"

You mean, Fortune thought, *if the Grand Master tells you it has to be done.*

"Sure, why not?" Fortune said. "But remember my price."

"I'll remember. Wait here."

Calhoun went into his study and dug into a humidor for

some money he kept there so his wife would not find it. He knew she searched the house for money when he wasn't home, but she'd never put her hand in there. She hated his cigars.

He came back into the living room and handed Al Fortune his money—double his usual fee. The man did not count it, he simply pocketed it.

"Thanks, Mayor."

"You don't want to count it?"

"Have I ever counted the money in front of you?" Fortune asked. "Have you ever cheated me?"

"No."

"Good night, Mr. Mayor," Fortune said. "Enjoy your supper. I'd join you, but you never invited me."

Before the mayor could say anything, Al Fortune turned on his heel and quickly left the house. Probably in a hurry to spend some of the money on beer.

When Fortune left the house, he took the money out and counted it. He always did that when he left the mayor. If the man ever shorted him, he'd march right back in and take it out of his hide. But it was all there.

Fortune wished he could be a fly on the wall when Calhoun talked to the Grand Master. He didn't know who the "Master" was, but he knew that Calhoun quaked in his boots when he talked about him.

Fortune walked back to town from the mayor's house, and thought about Clint Adams. He seemed to be a decent fella, but if Calhoun ever decided to pay the money, Fortune knew he'd kill Adams in a heartbeat. The legend of the Gunsmith had been around a long time, and he knew the man must be older than he appeared to be.

And he'd probably slowed down a lot over the years as well.

At least, Fortune hoped so.

• • •

As soon as Fortune left the house, Calhoun heard the creaking of the stairs. Seconds later, his wife appeared. Sturdy as a battleship, her once girlish figure totally gone, she stared at him disapprovingly—which was the only way she looked at him after thirty years of marriage.

"That was pitiful."

"You were eavesdropping, dear?" he asked.

"I don't eavesdrop in my own house, darling," she said. "I was giving you and your hired gun some privacy, but I couldn't help hear what was being said. Do you and your Grand Master think this Gunsmith is in town to cause trouble?"

"It's possible."

"Why would he bother with the likes of you?" she asked.

"We're a powerful organization, Martha."

"Oh, yes," she said, "in this town, but outside?"

"The Freemasons are known all over the world."

"Perhaps the Freemasons are," she said, "but the Knights of Misery?"

"Masonry, Martha," he corrected her, "the Knights of Masonry. Please don't use that . . . other name."

"Why?" she asked. "Isn't it accurate?"

"As usual, Martha, you don't know what you're talking about."

"And as usual, my dear husband," she said, "you have no spine. Enjoy your supper."

Martha Calhoun went back upstairs, leaving her husband standing there, fists clenched in impotent rage.

FIFTEEN

Clint met Harriet Willis in the lobby of the hotel. She was wearing a simple dress and had a shawl over her shoulders. Under the watchful eyes of Fred Anderson, Clint took her elbow and led her out to the street.

"What's with young Fred?" Clint asked. "He claims not to have a crush on you, but he was watching us like a hawk."

"You don't know about Fred," she said.

"I guess I don't."

"He works for the mayor," she said. "Yes, they think I don't know, but I do. The mayor sent him to me so I'd hire him and he could keep an eye on me and report back. So now he's probably already reported to the mayor on both of us."

"Why did you hire him if you knew that?" Clint asked her.

She shrugged and said, "I needed a clerk, and I'm not doing anything against the law, or against the tenets of the Masons. I don't care what the Freemasons—or Knights of Masonry, or Misery, or whatever they want to call themselves—do. It's not my concern as long as they leave me alone."

"If the mayor knows that, then why would he send someone to spy on you?"

She sighed and said, "We should talk about this when we're not on the street. May I choose the restaurant?"

"Please," he said. "I've had some bad food since I got to town."

"What's your pleasure?"

"Steak," he said, and kept himself from adding, "and you."

She smiled and said, "I know just the place."

Mayor Ben Calhoun knocked timidly on the front door of the big brick house. It was brand-new, with white pillars, a huge white front door, two stories high with large windows framed by very white shutters.

The door was opened by a black man wearing white gloves.

"Good evening, Cyrus," Calhoun said.

"Good evening, Mr. Mayor," the black servant said. "He's waitin' for you."

"Thank you."

The mayor entered, then paused while Cyrus closed and locked the door.

"This way, sir."

Calhoun knew the way, but also knew he was to never wander the halls of the house alone. No one got around the house without Cyrus leading the way.

Cyrus took him down two halls and led him into the library. All four walls were covered with books. One wall in particular was covered with books about the Masons, and also books written by authors who were Masons.

"He'll be down shortly, sir."

"Thank you, Cyrus."

The black man hesitated, then said, "Please don't touch nothing in the room."

"I won't, Cyrus," he said. "I've been here before, you know."

"Yes, sir."

Cyrus backed out of the room. Once, Calhoun had taken a book from the shelves, and caught hell for it. Now he knew just to walk around the room and study the titles while he waited for the Grand Master to arrive.

SIXTEEN

She took him to a busy restaurant where the people at the other tables either stared at them or actually spoke to her, greeting her by name.

"Okay," he said as they sat down, "the room seems to be cut in half."

She smiled.

"You mean half ignoring me and half saying hello?" she asked.

"What is that about?"

"Probably the same reason the mayor sent me a spy as a desk clerk. Let's order first. Steak?"

"With all the trimmings?"

The waiter came over and smiled at Harriet, greeting her by name and staring at her with cow eyes. He was a young man, and obviously infatuated. In fact, he was as young as Fred and he didn't seem to think she was too old to have a crush on.

"Welcome, Miss Willis," he said. "We haven't seen you here in a while."

"I've been busy, Sam, but I'm here now," she said. "This is my friend Mr. Adams."

The young man stared at Clint now, his eyes wide but nothing cow-eyed about them.

"So it's true?" he said.

"What's true?"

"You're really here, in Utopia?"

"I'm really here."

Sam seemed to realize what he was doing and shook his head.

"I'm sorry, Mr. Adams," he said, "Miss Willis. I didn't mean—"

"Nothing to be sorry about, Sam," Clint said. "Just feed me and you don't have to give it another thought. Okay?"

"Sure thing, Mr. Adams. What'll it be?"

Harriet Willis said, "Two steak dinners, Sam, with everything. And two cold beers."

"Comin' up, ma'am," he said, then looked at Clint and added, "sir."

"That's a smitten young man," Clint said. "Despite your age difference."

"Our age difference?"

"Well, I've been told you're too old to have a crush on."

"Oh? By who?"

"Fred."

"Oh, well, Fred works for me," she said, "and from time to time I have to . . . chastise him like today. So I'm sure he sees me more as a mother figure."

"Oh," Clint said, "I don't see anything motherly about you at all, Miss Willis."

"Well, I wouldn't want you to, Mr. Adams."

Clint turned his head, saw an older couple staring over at them. He smiled and waved and they averted their eyes.

"And who are they?"

"That's Judge Standish and his wife," she said. "She heads the Women's Committee for a Better Utopia."

"I thought Utopia was supposed to mean paradise," he said. "How could it get any better?"

"Eugenia Standish believes it would be a lot better without me."

"And why is that?"

Harriet smiled. "Probably for the same reason the mayor sent me a spy for a desk clerk."

"So the judge is a Mason?"

"Oh, yes."

"I see. Maybe it's time you told me a little about you and the people in this town."

"It's very simple," she said. "In the beginning, I saw no harm in the Freemasons having a chapter in town. It seemed good for the town."

"And then?"

"And then they became the Knights of Masonry, and then the Knights of Misery. They started . . . taking liberties, you might say."

"What kind of liberties?"

"They seemed to think as Masons—Knights—they shouldn't have to pay for anything in town. They used violence to make their point."

"Sounds like a gang of bullies to me."

"Exactly," she said. "They bought up businesses for pennies on the dollar, and closed all the churches down."

"And they tried to buy your business?"

"They did. I let it be known that I wouldn't sell, and also that I disapproved. I even spoke out against them."

"And what happened?"

"People stopped staying in my hotel," she said, "and I couldn't get anyone to work for me."

"And?"

"I shut up. People started to come back."

"And the mayor sent you a clerk/spy."

"Right, because I still couldn't get anyone to take the job."

"So you hired him."

"But I know what he's up to," she said, "so it doesn't matter."

"Harriet?"

"Yes."

"Is there a group in town that is against the Masons?" he asked.

"You mean like . . . rebels?"

"I guess that's what I mean."

Before she could answer, Sam arrived with steaming plates of steak and vegetables. He set the plates down in front of them, promised to return with the cold beers momentarily—and he did. They suspended their conversation until he was finished serving and was gone.

"Rebels," Clint reminded her.

"Why would you be interested in that, Clint?" she asked.

"Curiosity."

"What else are you curious about?"

"Well, how this steak tastes, for one."

"And?" she asked. He interpreted her look as suggestive, although that may not have been the way she meant it.

"We can get to that later," he said, and cut into his steak.

SEVENTEEN

"I have some new books," the Grand Master said from behind Mayor Calhoun.

"I noticed."

The man came up and stood next to him, pointed to the shelves.

"Some new Mark Twain," he said. "He's a Mason, you know."

"I, uh, knew," Calhoun lied.

"Other authors who are Masons," the Grand Master said, pointing. "Jonathan Swift, Oscar Wilde, this new British fella Arthur Conan Doyle. All Masons."

"Very impressive," Calhoun said.

"Yes, it is."

The Grand Master turned and walked to his desk. When he seated himself behind it, he was all business.

"What do you have for me, Benjamin?"

Calhoun was required to see the Grand Master once a week to fill him in on what was happening in town. It was a condition of Calhoun being "elected" mayor.

He sat opposite his leader and discussed several minor matters that had come up, and how he had handled them. The Master listened, with his fingertips pressed together.

"And your secretary—Esther, is it?" he asked when Calhoun was done.

"Um, yes?"

"She still works for you?"

"Yes."

"And you're still fucking her, Benjamin?"

"Well, uh, I'm, uh . . ." Calhoun stammered.

"Don't squirm, Benjamin," the Master said. "I hate it when you squirm. How is your wife?"

"She's, uh, fine."

"Lovely woman."

They both knew she was not, so Calhoun didn't say a word.

"And what else is on your mind, Mr. Mayor?"

"Else?"

"Come, come," the Grand Master said. "You've been chomping at the bit to tell me something ever since you arrived. What is it?"

"Well . . . a stranger arrived in town yesterday."

"Yes?"

"It occurred to me that he might be trouble."

"To the town, or to . . . us?"

"Oh, to us."

"And why would this stranger be trouble, Benjamin?" the leader asked.

"Um, well, his name is Clint Adams."

The Grand Master peered at Calhoun over his tented fingers.

"And should I know—oh, wait."

Calhoun did wait, remaining silent.

"Are we talking about . . . the Gunsmith?"

"Yes, sir."

"Interesting."

"Yes, sir."

"No, I mean, interesting that you think he would be trouble."

"I said he might be."

"Why would you think that?" the other man asked. "What might we have done to arouse his interest, or his ire?"

"Well . . . I don't know."

"Have you checked him out?"

"Yes, sir."

"And?"

"He appears to just be passing through."

"Well, then," the Grand Master said, "let him pass, Benjamin."

"Yes, sir."

"Do not even engage him unless it becomes . . . necessary."

"Yes, sir."

"And Benjamin?"

"Yes?"

"I'll decide when it becomes necessary."

"Yes, sir."

"In the meantime . . . who did you have check him out?"

"Al Fortune."

"Your personal gunman?"

"Yes."

"Well . . . have Mr. Fortune keep an eye on Mr. Adams for now."

"Yes, sir."

"Just an eye," the leader said. "As I said before, do not engage him. We do not wish to arouse his interest."

"Well . . . that's just it, sir."

"What's just it, Benjamin?"

"He's, uh, already been asking questions."

"Has he now?"

"Yes, sir."

The Grand Master dropped his hands and leaned forward to peer intently at Calhoun.

"You didn't tell me that before."

"No, sir."

"Why would you save that for last, Benjamin?"

"I, uh, well . . ."

"Never mind," the man behind the desk said. He sat back. "All right. Do we know who and what he's been asking?"

"Not exactly."

"Then let's find out."

"Yes, sir."

"That's all."

"Yes, sir."

Calhoun moved tentatively toward the door.

"Something else, brother?" the leader asked.

"Well . . . you don't think he could be here about what happened, do you?"

"What happened?"

"Yes, sir."

"No, Benjamin," the leader said. "I mean . . . what happened?"

It took Calhoun a moment, and then he said, "Uh, right, sir, yes. I understand. What, uh, happened?"

"That's all, Benjamin," the Grand Master said.

"Right, sir," Calhoun said, slinking out of the room, grateful that his wife didn't witness this particular meeting.

EIGHTEEN

"So, you haven't told me what makes you so curious about the Knights," Harriet told Clint over dessert.

"It's a fault of mine, being curious," he said. "Gets me into a lot of trouble."

"You might get into trouble here too if they hear that you're asking."

"Well, I guess they'll hear about it when Fred tells the mayor," he said. "That is, if he hasn't already told him."

"I'm sure he has."

"There's something you haven't told me yet too," he pointed out.

"Oh? What's that?"

"About the people in town who are against the Knights," Clint said. "Rebels, you called them?"

"No, you called them that."

"No," he insisted, "I think that was you."

"Well," she said, "whatever they're called, no one's been openly against the Knights in over a year."

"Too scared, huh?"

"Exactly."

"And the mayor? He's the head of this outfit, the Knights?"

"No one knows who the Grand Master is."

"The Grand Master?"

"That's what they call their leader."

"The Grand Master," Clint said again. "I guess that does sound pretty grand. But how come nobody knows who he is?"

"You have to be a member to know who the leader is," she said. "Nobody outside of the group has ever seen him."

"A man of mystery, huh?"

"Exactly."

"Seems like somebody would have taken steps to identify him by now," he said. "Maybe the sheriff?"

"Or you?" she asked. "Are you that curious?"

"I tell you what I would like to do," he said, "just out of curiosity, you understand."

"Of course."

"I'd like to talk to somebody who's not afraid to talk about the Knights," he said. "I wonder if there's anyone in town who could arrange that."

"You know," she said, "there just might be."

TWENTY

Now that they were in a hotel room and out of the public eye, Harriet told Clint, "There are quite a few people in town who oppose the Knights and what they've become. I can't say they're banded together, though. I'm sure they'd like to talk to you."

"Well," he said, "I'm not saying I want to be involved in organizing them, but—"

She turned her head and looked at him, lying next to her in her bed. She reached over and placed her hand on the naked hip.

"Clint, it's clear to me you're here for some reason," she said. "I'm not asking you what your purpose is, but maybe while you're here you can help."

"Are you involved with these people, Harriet?" he asked.

"Let's just say that if you were to get involved and organize these people, I might be willing to help. I truly think this town needs to get rid of the Knights before we become completely crushed beneath their thumb."

He reached down and took her hand.

"If you set it up, I'll meet with somebody."

She squeezed his hand, then rolled into his arm and put her head on his shoulder. They fell asleep that way.

Calhoun answered the knock at his door before it could wake his wife, who was sleeping upstairs. His own bedroom was on the first floor.

At the door was Judge Ambrose Standish.

"I got your message, Ben," Standish said. "What's going on?"

"Come inside, Judge."

Calhoun quietly relocked the door and led the judge to his study, where he closed that door.

"I don't want to wake Beatrice," he said. "Sit down. I'll get us some brandy."

Standish sat down, placing his hat in his lap. He took the glass of brandy, watched Calhoun seat himself behind his desk.

"Clint Adams is in town," Calhoun said then. "Do you know who Clint Adams is?"

"The Gunsmith," Standish said. "I'm not stupid, Benjamin."

"Never said you were, old friend." The two men were the same age, had come to Utopia at roughly the same time. Calhoun had been a lawyer before becoming mayor. Standish had been a judge for twenty years now. The judge was the only man the mayor felt he could speak freely to—more freely even than to any of their other Freemason brothers.

"He's staying at that woman's hotel."

"Harriet Willis?" Standish said with a sneer. "I saw her in a restaurant tonight with a man."

"It must have been him."

"What does he want in town?" Standish asked.

"I had Al Fortune ask him," Calhoun said. "He claims to just be passing through, but I don't know."

"What do you think he wants here?"

"I've been expecting something . . . someone . . ." Calhoun stammered, "ever since the, uh, incident with the government man."

"You think Clint Adams is a government man?"

"I don't know what he is," Calhoun said, "other than what his reputation says he is, but the Grand Master wants us to find out."

"Us?"

"All right, damn it, me. He wants me to find out," Calhoun said.

"Well, then, have your man pursue it further."

"I don't know if Fortune can handle this," Calhoun said. "It must be done subtly. It needs someone with brains."

"Well, that does leave Fortune out," Standish said, "and probably you too."

Calhoun laughed. Standish was the only man who could talk to him that way.

"So you want me to do it, huh?" the judge asked.

"You're in a position of authority."

"Not any more so than you."

"Well, as far as the law is concerned," Calhoun said, "you're the last word."

"Well, if we had a sheriff we could trust . . ." the judge said, letting it peter out.

"We both know that's not going to be the case for a while," Calhoun said. "Just find some pretext under which you can talk to him."

"Any suggestions?"

"If I had any ideas," Calhoun said, "I'd probably do it myself."

Standish finished his brandy, set the empty glass on the edge of the desk, and said, "I'll see what I can do."

TWENTY-ONE

In the morning he woke with Harriet's head between his legs. She was stroking his penis to life with her fingertips, and when she realized he was awake, she slid him into her eager mouth. Clint put his hands up over his head, gripped the bed rail, and moved his hips in unison with Harriet's bobbing head. She reached up to run her hands over his chest and belly while she worked his cock, wetting it thoroughly, slurping at times, until he felt his release building up in his legs. He lifted his hips and kept them elevated at the moment of release, and she took as much of him into her mouth as she could and didn't let him go until he was done. . . .

"Breakfast?" he asked her as he was getting dressed. He turned and looked at her over his shoulder. She was still naked in bed, making no move to get up.

"I think I just had breakfast," she said, and then blushed. "I don't know how you bring this out in me. I never talk like this."

"I know," he said. "And you never bring men back to your room. Now I know why."

74

"Oh? Why?"

He leaned over and kissed her.

"Because they'd never want to leave."

Judge Standish decided that the town might have a sheriff he didn't approve of, but that didn't mean he couldn't use him.

"Come into my chambers," he said to Sheriff Jim Gentile.

"I got a message that you needed to see me urgently, Judge," Gentile said, following the man in.

"Have a seat."

Standish seated himself in front of his wall of law books. He felt having those books towering over him was the proper background for him.

"I understand we have a visitor in town."

"Is that right?"

"Don't tell me a man like the Gunsmith can come to town and the local sheriff doesn't know about it."

"Oh, I know about it," Gentile said. "We already had a talk."

"Well, now, that's doing your job," the judge said. "What did he have to say for himself?"

"He just wanted to let me know he was in town."

"What's he doing in town?"

"Just passin' through, as far as I know."

"You two didn't talk about anything else?"

"Not that I remember. Why the interest, Judge?"

"Because he's the Gunsmith, that's why," Standish said. "Trouble, gunplay, and death follow him around wherever he goes."

"Probably through no fault of his own."

"Really? Is that your opinion?"

"Yep."

"Well, I tell you what," Standish said. "I'd like to form my own opinion."

"Talk to him yourself then."

"I'd like you to bring him to me so I can do just that."

"Bring him here?"

"That's right," Standish said. "If you do that, it'll carry weight as a legal inquiry."

Gentile studied the judge, wondering what the man was up to. Whatever it was, it had to involve the mayor, and if the two of them were involved, that meant so were the Knights of Misery.

"Bring him over today," Standish said, "this morning, in fact. I'll be right here going over some briefs."

Gentile hesitated, then said, "Well, okay." He stood up. "I'll see you a little later then."

Gentile caught Clint coming out of his hotel.

"Morning, Adams," he greeted.

"Sheriff," Clint said, coming up short. "What can I do for you?"

"Got someone who'd like to see you."

"Who's that?"

"Judge Standish."

"I saw him last night."

"You did? Where?"

"In a restaurant where Harriet Willis and I had supper."

"Well," Gentile said, "maybe that explains why he wants to see you."

"When does he want to do this?"

"Now," Gentile said, "this morning . . . but have you had breakfast yet?"

"No, I was just going—"

"Let's let the judge wait. Come on, I'll join you for a cup of coffee. We should talk."

TWENTY-TWO

"The mayor and the judge are cronies," Gentile told Clint, "going back before the Knights of Misery."

"Why would they jump on that bandwagon?"

"Because to them it looked like the only game in town."

"But they're not at the top of the heap," Clint said around his steak and eggs. "That would be the Grand Poobah."

"Master," Gentile said before he realized Clint was making a joke.

"And nobody knows who he is?"

"Nobody who isn't a member of the Knights," Gentile said.

"Have you ever tried to identify him?"

Gentile looked away and said, "No."

"Any guesses?"

"I could make a few," the lawman said, looking at Clint again, "but they'd be just that, guesses."

"Can I ask you something, Sheriff?"

"Go ahead," Gentile said. "I'll answer if I can."

"When the Knights took over," Clint said, "when they got the judge and the mayor, why did you stay?"

"Because I'll be damned if I'll let them push me out of office," Gentile said vehemently. "Oh, I'll leave when my term is up, but not until then. I can go to any other town and get a job. That's what I do. I'm a lawman."

"Won't it irk you to leave the town in their hands?" Clint asked.

The lawman looked around the small café. They were at a corner table, where they could not be overheard.

"There are people in this town who will fight to get it back," he said. "I just don't know if I can wait that long."

"When's your term up?"

"Eight months."

"And you don't see anything happening before then?" Clint asked.

"Not in this town," Gentile said. "Not unless they find someone to lead them."

"Why not get in touch with the Federal Government?" Clint asked. "Work with them."

"Because I don't know who's a Mason and who's not," Gentile said. "Or who is a Knight. Once they were the same, but now the line's blurred."

"So you'd rather ride out?"

"If nothing happens in the next eight months? Damned right."

"So why warn me about the judge?"

"Talk is cheap," Gentile said, "and that's all I'm doin'. Talkin'." He drank his coffee and stood up. "The rest is up to the town, and whoever they find to lead them. Come to my office when you're ready to see the judge and I'll walk you over."

The man left before Clint could ask why he didn't lead them himself. He could ask him when he went to his office, but he decided not to. He finished his breakfast, had some more coffee, and then walked to the sheriff's office.

• • •

Gentile knocked on the door of the judge's chambers and opened it without waiting for a reply.

"Judge?"

Standish looked up from what he was doing.

"Mr. Adams is here."

"Bring him in, Sheriff, bring him in." He stood up. "Make the introduction." He buttoned his jacket over his vest.

Gentile allowed Clint to enter first and followed.

"Judge Standish, this is Clint Adams," he said. "Adams, Judge Standish."

"Welcome to Utopia, son," Standish said, sticking out his hand.

"Thank you, sir." Clint shook the judge's hand, releasing it as soon as he could. It was like shaking hands with a skeleton.

"I saw you in the restaurant last night with Miss Willis, but had no idea who you were."

"Likewise."

"Can I offer you some coffee?"

"No, thanks," Clint said. "I just had a couple of pots with my breakfast."

"All right then. Have a seat, please."

The man walked around behind his desk, but before he sat down, he dismissed the sheriff.

"That'll be all, Sheriff Gentile," he said. "Thank you."

"Yes, sir."

Clint looked over his shoulder at the man and they exchanged a glance before the lawman left. As the door closed, he turned back and looked at the man behind the desk.

TWENTY-THREE

"I understand from the sheriff that you're just passing through our fair town," Judge Standish said.

"I don't know how fair your town is, Judge, but that's true enough."

Standish frowned.

"You don't like our town?"

"I probably would have liked a town called Beldon," Clint said, deciding to be as truthful as he could with the man. "I don't really think too much of the town called Utopia."

"Would you mind telling me why?"

"Well, for one, let me say I don't much like the way the town got its new name."

"You've been listening to stories, Mr. Adams," the judge said. "I would think a man with a reputation to live down—a reputation I'm sure has been . . . shall we say, embellished—would understand about stories."

"Suppose you tell me the real story then," Clint suggested. "One that doesn't involve a pack of bullies called the Knights of Masonry."

"Bullies?" the judge asked. "The Knights are Freemasons,

sir. Freemasons are hardly bullies. Some of our greatest leaders, and authors, and artists have been Freemasons."

"But how many of them have been Knights of Misery?" Clint asked.

The judge bristled.

"Where did you hear that name?"

"Around."

"From people in this town?"

"A few."

"If there are people in this town who are dissatisfied with the way it's being run, they should attend the monthly town council meetings and voice their disapproval there, not on the streets."

"Maybe they're afraid to."

"Sir," the judge said, "I'm really not sure you should be judging an entire town based on what a few miscreants have to say."

"Seems to me the miscreants in this town are members of a group run by a man who won't show his face."

"Sir!" The judge brought his hand down on the desk, like a gavel. "I won't have talk like that. I am a proud member of the Freemasons."

"So, I understand, is the mayor."

"What of it?"

"You fellas ought to stick to running your little club and let other people worry about running the town, don't you think?"

"No, sir, I do not. But I'm not here to defend the Masons against you."

"Why are we here, Judge?"

"I want to know what you are doing in town."

"Passing through."

"And if you don't like it, why not move on?" the man asked.

"Oh, I'll move on . . . eventually."

"When?"

"When my horse is well rested enough."

"I would suggest you make that soon."

"Are you telling me to get out of town, Judge?" Clint asked. "I haven't broken any laws."

"You don't know our laws, sir."

"I thought the law was the law, Judge," Clint said. "Are you telling me that Utopia has its own laws? Or is it the Knights of Misery who have their own?"

"I've asked you not to use that name!"

"I know you have," Clint said, "but to me, it seems to fit." He stood up. "Are we done with you warning me off? Why aren't you having your town sheriff do it? Oh, wait, he's not a Mason, is he?"

"You are deliberately being offensive, sir," the judge said. "Makes me wonder why. What are you after?"

"Me? Like I told you, Judge, I'm just after a little rest for me and my horse. But I can't help making some observations while I'm in town."

"And what would you do with those observations?"

"I don't know," Clint said. "I guess that depends on who asks me. Good day, Judge."

Clint left, leaving Judge Standish totally unhappy with the meeting they'd had. Standish didn't know what he was going to tell his friend the mayor so that he could pass it on to the Grand Master.

He'd learned little or nothing from the Gunsmith, except for the fact that the man did not like the Knights of Masonry.

In that he was not alone.

But he alone was dangerous.

TWENTY-FOUR

Clint found the sheriff waiting for him outside the building. He fell in next to him and they walked away together.

"What'd you tell him?"

"Maybe too much," Clint said, and relayed his conversation to the lawman.

"The judge won't do anything," Gentile said. "He's got no power here, but he may tell someone else who will do something."

"The Grand Master?"

"Not directly. He'll tell the mayor, and then *he'll* tell the Grand Master."

"Okay," Clint said. He stopped, looked around, then pulled the lawman into an alley. "I've heard stories about the Knights of Misery, but nothing specific. Do they have guns to send after me? Will they try to kill me, or scare me off?"

"They've got members who will do whatever they're told," Gentile said. "They've got some men who can handle guns. They usually work in groups, though, intimidating people that way."

"Give me a for instance."

"They wanted to own the general store. They went in there three and four at a time, every day, scaring customers off and destroying merchandise until the owner sold—for pennies on the dollar."

"But they didn't kill anyone."

"No."

"Now here's the important question," Clint said. "Have they killed anyone?"

Gentile hesitated, then said, "Well, there's no proof, but—"

"Tell me what you think, Sheriff."

"I don't think," Gentile said. "I know they've killed people, but I can't prove it. See, folks have just . . . disappeared."

"Like who?"

"Merchants who didn't want to sell," the lawman said, "and a while back there was a fella came to town, a stranger like you. He started asking questions, and then . . . one morning he was gone."

"He didn't leave?"

"I checked the livery," Gentile said. "His horse was there in the morning, but then in the afternoon it had disappeared."

"So whoever killed him didn't get rid of the horse fast enough."

"Right."

"So the Knights have got at least one killer in their midst," Clint said. "Who would that be, Sheriff?"

"I can think of a couple of fellas who might fill the bill," Gentile said. "Jack Cole is a youngster, about twenty, who will do anything the Knights tell him. In fact, there are a few youngsters like that in town who want to be Knights."

"Like Fred Anderson, over at the hotel?"

"Sure, Fred wants to join, but he'd never kill anyone. Worst he'll do is spy for the mayor."

"Which he's doing to Harriet, only she knows about it," Clint said.

"Does she? I was hoping she did. She's a pretty smart gal."

"Who else?" Clint asked. "Tell me who I have to be on the lookout for."

"Well, Al Fortune, for one," Gentile said.

"I've already talked with him," Clint said. "I figured him for some kind of money gun."

"Yeah, Al will do anything for money, but he doesn't want to have anything to do with the Knights. He works for the mayor."

"And who else?"

"There's a fella who is a Knight himself, does dirty work for them. Gathers up the men who will do damage and scare people, but him . . . he's a killer. I know it and I can't prove it."

"Who is it?"

"Zack Franklin," Gentile said.

"Handle a gun?"

"Likes to work at close range," the lawman said. "I'd say deadly with a knife, good with a gun."

"Back shooter?"

"Definitely. That wouldn't bother him at all."

"What's he look like?"

"Tall, solid, ugly scar that sort of twists one eyebrow and eyelid. Surprised he didn't lose that eye."

"Okay," Clint said.

"Now I got a question."

"What?"

"Why not just leave town?" Gentile asked. "If you think they're gonna send somebody after you, why not just go?"

Clint thought just for a moment about telling the truth, but then decided to fall back on his reputation.

"If I let myself get run out of a town, the word would get around. I'd be defending myself everywhere I went."

"Don't you do that anyway?"

"It would escalate if the word got out that I could be scared off."

"I see what you mean."

"Now I've got another question."

"Okay."

"If push comes to shove," Clint said, "and they do come after me, where will you stand?"

Gentile tapped the tin star on his chest.

"I stand where I always stand," he said. "Right behind this."

"That's good enough for me," Clint said.

"What're you gonna do now?" the sheriff asked.

"I've got somebody to talk to," Clint said, "somebody who might give me a name—that is, unless you want to give me one."

"The name of who?"

"Anybody who'll take a stand against the Knights."

Gentile rubbed his jaw.

"That's a tough one, Adams," the lawman said. "I'll have to give it some thought."

"You do that," Clint said, "and when you come up with somebody, the name's Clint."

TWENTY-FIVE

Clint went back to the hotel, where Fred was still behind the desk. He looked sleepy enough to fall asleep on his feet.

"Don't you ever go home?" he asked.

"Miss Willis hasn't been able to hire another clerk," he said. "I'm waiting for her to relieve me."

"I'll check on her," Clint said. "I happen to know she went to sleep late."

Fred shrugged, placed his elbow on the desk and his head into his hand.

Clint went around behind the desk and walked down the hall to Harriet's room. He knocked on the door, then knocked again. He expected her to answer the door wrapped in a sheet, but when she did open the door, she was fully dressed.

"Well, back for more?" she asked, then blushed.

"More talk, I'm afraid," he said. "Also, your friend at the desk is asleep on his feet."

"Yes, I know," she said. "I'm supposed to let him go home to bed. Can we talk out there?"

"Sure," he said, "as long as we're alone."

"Whatever you have in mind, can we do it at the desk?" she asked.

"Like I said," Clint replied, "I'm interested in talk."

"Then let's go and let poor Fred go home—if he will," she added.

"You think he'll stay to do some spying?"

"Maybe."

"I don't think he's faking," Clint said. "He's out on his feet."

She came out into the hall, closed the door, and they walked up to the desk.

"Time to go home, Fred," she said. "See you tomorrow."

Fred jumped, lifted his head, and asked, "You won't need me this evening?"

"I don't think so," she said. "We don't have that many guests. Go home, get some sleep, and come back tomorrow morning."

"Yes, ma'am." Fred looked at Clint, but didn't say anything. He quit the desk, walked across the lobby, and left. Clint walked to the door and peered out. Fred was walking away, crossing the street. Satisfied that the boy wasn't eavesdropping, he went back to the desk, where Harriet had taken up residence.

"Is he gone?" she asked.

"Yep."

"What's on your mind then?"

"I had a talk this morning with both the sheriff and the judge."

"Judge Standish?"

"Yep."

"What did he want?"

Clint gave her a brief account of the conversation, and by the time he was done she looked worried.

"I think you're in danger, Clint," she said. "The judge is sure to tell the mayor—"

"—and he'll go to the Grand Master. Yeah, I figured that."

"You're deliberately setting yourself up as a target?" she asked.

"Well, that wasn't my plan when I woke up this morning, but yeah, that seems to be what I did."

"But why? Why are you even so interested?"

Clint hesitated, wondered if what he was about to do was wise, then decided to go ahead and do it.

TWENTY-SIX

They were alone in the lobby, no one was eavesdropping, so he told her what he was really doing there.

"You're working for the government?"

"They're concerned about what these Knights of Misery might try next," he said, not telling her about the assassination possibilities.

"Why are you telling me this?" she asked. "Do you trust me that much?"

"As a matter of fact, I do," he said. He didn't bother telling her that he thought he was already in as much danger as he could be. If they were going to try to kill him for asking questions, they'd go ahead and kill him for working for the government.

"I—I don't know what to say."

"Well, I have a suggestion," he said. "Arrange for me to talk with someone."

"You mean, somebody who's against the Knights?" she asked.

"That's exactly what I mean."

"I could do that," she said. "But . . . what should I tell them? I mean . . . how much?"

"Just who I am and that I want to talk," he said. "Maybe by tonight?"

"I—I'll try," she said. "I—I'd probably have to leave the hotel for a while to do it."

"I don't want to cost you business," he said, "but I would like to do this as soon as possible. If I'm in danger, I need to know if I can count on anyone to back me up."

"You mean . . . with guns?"

"That's exactly what I mean."

Judge Standish walked into his friend Ben Calhoun's office and sat down in a chair.

"What's wrong, Judge?"

"I think we're going to have a problem with Clint Adams."

"What happened?"

"He was offensive and belligerent," the judge said. "He won't back down."

"Did you find out why he's here?" the mayor asked.

"He still insists he was just passing through," Standish said.

"Then why won't he keep going?"

"He says he doesn't like what he's hearing about the Masons. Ben, we'll have to get rid of him."

"We can't make that decision, Judge," Calhoun said. "I'll have to check with the Master."

"I don't think he's going to see any other option," Standish said.

"I'll tell him what you said, Judge."

"This killing . . ." the judge said, trailing off.

"What?"

"It's not what I had in mind when I joined the Masons."

Calhoun looked around, as if he expected someone to be listening. He got up, went to the door, looked outside. Esther was sitting there alone, seemingly unconcerned about what was being said in his office. He closed the door, locked it, and went back to his desk.

"Judge, don't say things like that where people can hear," he advised.

"I know that, Ben," Standish said. "I'm not an idiot."

"Well, then, don't say stuff like that to me either," the mayor said.

"Are you going to turn me in?"

"Of course not," Calhoun said without much conviction in his voice. "We're old friends."

"Well, tell me then," Standish said. "When you joined the Masons, did you expect them to become the Knights of Misery?"

"Don't say that!" Calhoun snapped.

Standish sighed, stood up.

"Okay, fine, Ben," he said. "We'll just continue to turn a blind eye to everything."

"Judge, you're the one who says we should get rid of Adams," Calhoun reminded him.

"That's because I'm in too deep, Benjamin," Standish said, "as are you."

Calhoun rushed around from behind the desk and put his hand on his friend's shoulder. They walked to the door that way.

"Judge," Calhoun said, lowering his voice, "just don't say or do anything . . ."

"What?" Standish asked. "Stupid? Don't worry, Ben. Like I said, we're in too deep to turn back now."

Calhoun unlocked his door and let the judge out, stood in the doorway, and watched him leave.

"What's wrong with the judge?" Esther asked.

"What? Nothing. Why do you ask?"

"He just doesn't seem to be himself."

"He's fine," Calhoun said, "just fine."

She looked up at her boss.

"Do you want me to come inside?"

"No, not now," he said. "Maybe later, Esther."

He backed into his office, closed the door . . . and Esther heard the lock turn again.

TWENTY-SEVEN

Clint spent the afternoon at The Whiskey. He got a beer from the bartender, Bud Cook, then found his way to a back table from which he could see the entire room.

He had told Harriet that was where he'd be, but she'd said, "Whoever I find to meet you, I don't think they're going to want to do it in public."

"That's fine," Clint said. "Just have them step into the saloon, stop just inside the doors, look around, and then step out again. I'll follow."

"What if somebody does that and it's not the person I send?"

"Just tell them to go to the nearest alley when they leave. I'll meet them there."

"Okay," she said. "I hope . . . just be careful."

"I will."

And part of being careful was sitting where he could see the whole saloon.

He was low on his beer when the bartender came over with a bar rag over his shoulder.

"Another one?"

"Why not? And you can take the rest of this one."

Bud Cook removed the remainder of the warm beer, went and got a cold one, and brought it back.

"Not much action going on," Clint said.

"It's not that kind of town," Cook said. "There's been no gamblin' since the Masons came to town and became the Knights."

"What about women?"

"No saloon girls," Cook said, "but I could find you a whore if you really wanted one."

"No, that's okay."

"So, you waitin' for somebody?"

"I'm just killing time, Bud," Clint said.

"I can see that," Cook said, "I'm just wonderin' why you're doin' it in this town."

"Good as any other, I guess."

"That's where you're wrong, but it's your call. Wave when you want another one."

Clint nodded. He had noticed the absence of girls working the saloon floor earlier, but it hadn't dawned on him that it was because of the Freemasons. No churches, no girls, no gambling—what was the point, he wondered.

"Back so soon, Benjamin?" the Grand Master asked.

"I, uh, got the information you wanted, brother," Calhoun said.

They were standing in front of the bookshelves again.

"All right then, have a seat," the man said. "Tell me what's on your mind."

"Still Clint Adams," Calhoun said. "Judge Standish had a talk with him this time."

"Any new information?"

"He still insists that he was just passing through when he got here," Calhoun said, "but the judge thinks he might be trouble now."

"Why is that?"

"Adams says he doesn't like what he sees in this town," the mayor said.

"Then he should leave."

"Well, he isn't," Calhoun said.

"What's he going to do?"

"We don't know for sure," Calhoun said. "He, uh, wouldn't say."

The Grand Master drummed his fingers on his desk as he thought.

"All right," he said. "We'll have to do something."

"Do you want me to get Al Fortune?"

"No," the Master said, "Fortune is not one of us."

"Th-then who do you want to—"

"You know who," the Master said, cutting him off.

"Not Franklin."

"Yes, Zack Franklin."

"But he's . . . uncontrollable."

"I can control him," the Master said. "All you have to do is find him and send him here."

"Um, is it okay if I have Al Fortune do that?" Calhoun asked.

"Yes, fine," the other man said. "I'm aware that Zack Franklin scares the wits out of you, Mr. Mayor. By all means, send Fortune for him."

"Yes, sir," Calhoun said. "I'll get right on it."

"Have him come here after dark," the Master said. "He knows. . . ."

"Yes, sir."

"And Ben."

"Yes?"

"What kind of shape is the judge in?"

"He's fine." Calhoun swallowed. "Why?"

"I have my eye on him," the other man said. "That's all."

The mayor hesitated.

"That's all," the Grand Master said again. "Go."

TWENTY-EIGHT

Clint was on his third beer when a man walked through the batwing doors, looked around the room, then backed out again. It seemed a very natural act, someone looking for someone and not finding them. It could even have gone unnoticed, there were that few men in the saloon as it was still just late afternoon. Clint had started to wonder if he'd have to sit there all day until dark.

He stood up, waved at the bartender as he went by—also very natural—and walked outside. He looked left and right, saw an alley to his right. He waited for some people to pass by and when he thought he was not being watched, turned right and went down the alley.

There was no one in the alley, but it went all the way through to the back of the saloon. He walked to the back, found the man waiting by the back door of the saloon.

"In here," the man said, and opened the door. Clint wondered how he had access to that door, unless it was always left unlocked.

And he thought, just briefly, as the man went inside, that this might be a trap. If it was, it would mean Clint had trusted the wrong person when he trusted Harriet.

No, he still felt she was trustworthy, so he followed the man through the door.

Once inside, the man struck a match, touched it to an oil lamp hanging on a post.

"Close the door," the man said. "Lock it."

Clint did so, turned to face the man. He was tall, in his thirties, wasn't wearing a gun, dressed cleanly. Clint had the feeling he wore an apron over his clothes every day. A storekeeper if he ever saw one.

"My name is Alex Lincoln," the man said. "You're Mr. Adams?"

"That's right, Clint Adams."

Lincoln came forward and extended his hand. Clint shook it.

"Harriet told me I could trust you," he said. "If I can't, and you go to the Knights, I'm dead."

"I don't have any intention of going to the Knights," Clint said.

Alex Lincoln rubbed his hand over his mouth, then removed his hat.

"Harriet said you wanted to talk to someone who was against the Knights," he said. "Why?"

"Because I'm against them," Clint said. "I'm against what they've done to this town."

"They've shackled us," Alex said. "Those of us who have businesses that they haven't taken over can't afford to leave. It's only a matter of time until they will want to take over."

"Tell me, Alex," Clint said, looking out the back window. "How many more men in town feel the way you do?"

"A lot," he said. "Probably half the town."

"That sounds like a good amount," Clint said. "Why not fight? Kick them out of town?"

"Because we're storekeepers, Mr. Adams, not gunmen,"

Alex said. "On the other hand, if we could hire you—or someone like you—"

"Bring in some hired guns and you might fall under *their* control in the end," Clint said. "That's not the way to go."

Alex looked around, saw a box, went over, and sat down on it.

"So tell me then, which is the way to go?" he asked. "How do we get out from under them?"

"You do it yourselves," Clint said.

"We can't," Alex said. "We've talked about it. We can't go against their guns."

"How many of the Knights actually wear guns?" Clint asked.

"They seem to use the same four or five gunmen," Alex said.

"And do they announce when they come in that they represent the Knights?"

"Oh, yes, very proudly."

"You know any of them by name?"

"Most of them," Alex said. "They were here already when the Knights came."

"So, they didn't bring gunmen with them?"

"They brought one."

"And who was that?"

"Zack Franklin," Alex said. "That man is a killer, through and through."

"So other than him, they use locals?"

"Yes," Alex said, "locals who seem to believe everything the Knights tell them."

"Alex," Clint said, "I want to help."

"I know your reputation, Mr. Adams, but what can you do? You're one man."

"You have a store?"

"Yes," Alex said. "I have a feed store. I've had it for several years. Before that I worked for other people in town."

"Can we talk there instead of here?"

"I guess," Alex said carefully, "but . . . not until after dark."

"And can I talk to some others at the same time?" Clint asked.

"You want to have a meeting?" Alex asked. "Is that it?"

"How many others can you round up?"

"Probably more by using your name."

"Then use it," Clint said. "Set something up for tonight and I'll be there."

Alex stood up.

"My store is on Third Street, just off Front," he said. "Come around back about nine o'clock, knock once. I'll let you in."

"How many others do you think you can get?" Clint asked.

"I'm not sure," Alex said. "I think maybe you and me will find that out at the same time."

TWENTY-NINE

Al Fortune didn't mind being sent to find Zack Franklin. If the Knights wanted that kind of dirty work done, that was Franklin's specialty. Since he came to town, everyone had discovered what kind of man he was, and steered clear. Even Fortune, who didn't mind killing for profit, did not enjoy it the way Zack did.

On the other hand, the only man in town that Zack Franklin seemed to have any use for was Al Fortune.

Fortune knew where to find Zack. There was a whorehouse at the southern end of town that the Knights hadn't closed down. In fact, some of the Knights even used it.

Fortune entered, and was greeted by the buxom madam, a woman about ten years past being a whore herself. Still, she might have been worth a poke just for her experience. In Fortune's own experience at the whorehouse, some of the girls tended to just lie there.

"Hello, Al," Carly said. "Come to try out one of the new girls?"

"You got new girls?"

"Two," she said. "One Mexican and one Chinese."

Al made a face.

"Don't want no Chinee gal, but I might try the Mexican. She a spitfire?"

"You've told me you like girls who move," she said. "Baby, this gal moves."

"Maybe later, Carly. Right now I'm lookin' for Zack Franklin."

Her face darkened.

"Him."

"Yeah, him. Is he here?"

She jerked her chin.

"He's got the new Chinese gal upstairs," she said. "I never know if I'm gonna ever get my girl back alive when he's around."

"What room?"

"Five."

"I'll see if I can save her."

"You do that," she said. "And maybe you can get him to leave with you."

"That's kinda what I had in mind, Carly," he said. "Do my best."

As he started past her, she put her hand on his arm. He looked down at her hand; then his eyes were drawn to her chubby, powdered cleavage.

"You get him to leave," she said, "and you can have a free poke with any gal here—including me."

"Like I said, Carly," he replied. "I'll do my best."

Upstairs, the Chinese girl, Mei Ling, was wondering if she was going to get out of this room alive.

First, Zack Franklin was a big man, and she was barely five feet tall. Next, he had a huge penis, which was swaying back and forth in front of her.

"Go on," he said. "Take it in yer mouth. Suck it!" he commanded.

Carly had told Mei Ling that she wouldn't have to do

this sort of thing for a while, not until she got broken in. Then, when this man picked her, the madam pulled her aside and said, "Do whatever he wants."

Zack reached down, took hold of one of her chocolate brown nipples, and twisted it.

"You gonna do like I say? Suck it!"

Mei Ling eyed the purple-veined monster with trepidation, and almost fainted from relief when there was a knock at the door. Probably a momentary reprieve, but she accepted it.

"Whoever that is better have a damned good reason for interruptin' me," Zack shouted as he headed for the door.

THIRTY

Clint went back to the hotel, found Harriet behind the desk.

"Did he show up?" she asked, lowering her voice even though they were alone.

"Yes," Clint said, "and we're meeting later with some other people."

"Really?" Her eyes widened. "You must have impressed him."

"I think the people of this town are fed up," Clint said. "They just don't know what to do about it."

"I'd say that's exactly right. They need a leader, and that could be you."

"No," Clint said, "the leader has to come from within. Maybe it could be Alex."

"He's a storekeeper."

"A lot of them might be storekeepers," Clint said. "They're going to have to learn to solve their own problems, though."

"And you can teach them that?"

"That," he said, "I can do."

• • •

When Zack opened the door to Room Five, his erect penis preceded him. Fortune jumped back.

"Hey, watch it with that!"

Zack took a step back so that his dick wasn't sticking out into the hall. Fortune tried not to look. Instead, he looked past Zack at the Chinese girl on her knees by the bed. She was naked, with long black hair, pert, chocolate-tipped breasts, and frightened eyes, and he felt nothing. He didn't like Chinese girls.

"Zack, they want you."

"Who wants me?" Zack asked.

"You know . . . them. The Knights."

"The Grand Master?"

"That's right."

"Tell 'im to wait," the man said. "I'm a little busy. This pretty little Chinee girl's gonna suck my cock."

"Her?" Fortune asked. "She'd never get her mouth open wide enough."

"You wanna bet?" Zack asked. "You wanna bet I can get it in her mouth, and then in her bum?"

"Never happen."

"How much?"

Zack backed up and Fortune entered the room, putting his hand in his pocket for his money. They didn't want Zack to come over until after dark anyway.

Clint stayed in his room until dark, then left and went down to the lobby. Harriet was still at the desk and she waved him over.

"Please be careful," she said. "In the beginning people tried to have secret meetings, but the Knights always found out and showed up."

"Well, let's hope Alex has only been talking to people he can really trust."

"It's very hard to decide who to trust and who not to trust since the Masons came to town."

"You know, I've never asked this, but where do the Masons meet?"

"There's a new building about two blocks from City Hall. They call it a temple, but it's just a big, empty building."

"I'll have to take a look at it. How often do they meet?"

"Once a week."

"Do you know what day?"

"Friday, I think."

Three days. If nobody was there, maybe he could get a look at it tonight, after the meeting. Maybe even get inside.

"Please come back here when you're done," she said, touching his arm. "I need to know you're all right."

"Don't worry," he said, "I'll be back."

Al Fortune and Zack Franklin came down the stairs, Fortune's money in Zack's pocket. From upstairs, the screaming Mei Ling had been doing when Zack stuck his enormous dick up her ass still echoed—or seemed to. Fortune had never seen anything like it before.

As Zack went out the front door, Carly grabbed Fortune's arm.

"Is my girl alive?"

"She's alive," Fortune assured her. "A little sore, but alive."

He followed Zack out.

THIRTY-ONE

Clint worked his way around to the back of Alex Lincoln's feed store and knocked on the back door. After a few moments, the door opened and Alex appeared.

"Come on in," he said.

He stepped aside to let Clint enter, then locked the door.

"How many people are here?" Clint asked.

"Come and see."

He led Clint through the darkened back room into another small room that served as an office. There were five other people there. Three men about Alex's age, and an older man who looked to be dozing. But it was the fifth person who surprised Clint. She was in her late twenties, tall and slender, except for a full bust, with a wild cascade of red hair. She had been staring at the floor with her arms folded, but lifted her head as Alex and Clint entered, so that Clint was able to see her flashing green eyes. He also noticed the well-cared-for gun she wore on her left hip.

"This is all?" he asked.

"Everyone else is too scared," the girl said. "So you're Clint Adams?"

"That's right."

She stepped forward and extended her hand.

"Rita O'Doyle."

"Happy to meet you," Clint said, shaking her hand. "Can you use that gun?"

She smiled. Her mouth was wide, her teeth white, and all the muscles in her face seemed to cooperate with the smile.

Her eyes crinkled and she said, "Better than most men."

"Clint, let me introduce you to the rest of the folks here," Alex said. "This is Jake Heller, he owns and runs the hardware store; Charlie Tolbert, the livery."

"Tolbert," Clint said, switching his hand from Heller's to the liveryman's. "Saw you when I came to town."

"That horse of yours is a dream," Tolbert said. "Never saw an animal so well behaved."

"Any more trouble with that fella Wayne?"

Tolbert laughed and said, "Always."

"You met Paul Wayne?" Alex asked.

Clint looked at Charlie.

"Wayne was givin' me a hard time when Mr. Adams rode in."

"Is Wayne for or against?" Clint asked.

"We'll talk about him later," Alex said, and continued with the introductions. The third man was Mark Guthrie, who owned one of the smaller saloons in town, and the older man was Hector Williams.

"I was told there'd be whiskey," he said as Clint shook his sandpaper-dry hand.

"Here ya go, Heck," Rita said, and produced a pint bottle.

"And what do you do, Rita?"

"I work for Alex," she said. "I drive his wagons."

"She's kept me from being robbed more times than I can count," Alex said.

"Sounds like a handy woman to have around."

"In more ways than you know, Gunsmith," Rita said.

The old man was making sucking noises as he worked at the bottle. For all intents and purposes, Clint was talking to five people.

"I tried to get more to come," Alex said. "They don't trust you."

"What about you?" Clint asked.

"These are the people who trusted me enough to come," he said.

"We're storekeepers, Mr. Adams," Mark Guthrie said. "Merchants. How do we fight back against these gunmen?"

"And zealots," Heller said. "There ain't nothin' worse than a religious zealot. They're crazy!"

"I understood that these Knights were not about religion," Clint said.

"They closed down all the churches," Charlie said. "That's got to do with religion, ain't it?"

"Let's all settle down and see what Mr. Adams has in mind," Alex suggested.

"Yeah," Rita said, hands on her hips, "I'd like to hear what Mr. Gunsmith has on his mind."

With her standing there that way, hip-shot, a saucy look on her face, and a gun on her hip, Clint could not tell them what he had on his mind at that moment.

Across town, Zack Franklin knocked on the back door of the Grand Master's house. The door was opened by Cyrus, whose white-gloved hands almost gleamed in the dark when the moonlight hit them.

"This way, Mr. Zack."

Following the black man, Zack told Cyrus, "I thought I told you not to call me Mr. Zack."

"Sorry, suh," Cyrus said. "It's a hard habit to break."

For some reason Cyrus, aside from Al Fortune, was the only man in town Zack had any liking for.

Zack smiled as he followed the black man down the

dark halls of the house. He had Fortune's money in his pocket, and the cries of the Chinese girl as he brutally fucked her ass still echoed in his head. If the girl hadn't been broken in before, she sure as hell was now.

"He'll be down shortly," Cyrus said, letting Zack into the library.

Zack wondered why the Grand Master was never in the library already waiting for him. He wondered if he kept everyone waiting when he had a meeting with them.

He studied the books on the wall, just for something to do. He didn't like books. He didn't understand them. How could someone sit still long enough to write down all those words? The Master had once told Zack that books were meant to educate people.

Zack Franklin's way of educating people was to hurt them. He hoped the Grand Master had sent for him for just that reason.

He was ready to educate somebody real bad!

THIRTY-TWO

"Actually," Clint said, "I was more hoping to hear what you folks had in mind."

"Us?" Heller said.

"Whataya mean?" Charlie asked. "You called this meetin'."

"I know I did, but it was to find out how long you folks were going to put up with this situation."

"Until somebody comes along who can fix it, that's how long," Guthrie said.

"You're talkin' to the wrong crowd, Mr. Gunsmith, if you're lookin' for men who are ready to fight. This bunch ain't got a pair of *cojones* between 'em."

"Shut up, Rita," Guthrie said. "Just because you wish you was a man—"

"I'm already more man than any of you," she snapped back.

Clint was beginning to see the problem clearly. There was no way anybody could accomplish anything if they were unable to work together.

"Okay, hold on!" he shouted. "Quiet down. You're not going to get anywhere fighting among yourselves. If anything is going to happen, you're going to have to cooperate."

"Do you see how many people showed up for this meeting?" Heller asked. "What do you think we can accomplish?"

"Six people can accomplish a lot more than one," Clint said.

"We're not gunmen," Heller said.

"We can't use a gun," Guthrie said.

"Speak for yourselves," Rita said, slapping her holster. "I can use a gun just fine."

Clint looked at Alex as Rita and the men began to bicker again. Alex shrugged, as if to say, "It's gonna be a long night."

Zack turned as he heard footfalls behind him. The Grand Master entered the library, wearing a robe that was belted around the waist. It was maroon-colored and the material seemed to reflect the light from the lamp. Zack had never seen a garment like it before.

"Still not interested in books, Zack?"

"No, sir." Zack didn't particularly like the Grand Master, but he respected him. How could you not respect a man who had an entire town beneath his thumb, and they didn't even know it was him grinding them into the dirt? You had to admire a man like that. And he paid enough to keep Zack's silence.

"Have a seat, my boy," the Master said. "I really wish I could get you interested in reading. Perhaps the work of the Marquis de Sade would do." He almost seemed to be speaking to himself. "Yes, I shall have to try and get a copy of that."

"Marky who?"

"Never mind."

The Grand Master shrugged his shoulders. It was his way of going on to his next subject.

"I've got a little task for you, my boy."

"Your little tasks are always fun for me," Zack said. "And profitable."

"This is something Al Fortune wanted to take on very badly," the Master said. "But I insisted we give it to you."

"Al's okay," Zack said. "Why not give it to him?"

"Because it's too big for him," the Grand Master said. "This is the kind of thing that only you can handle."

"Well, then, it must be big," Zack said. "Who do I get to kill?"

"Does the name Clint Adams mean anything to you?"

THIRTY-THREE

"Unless you're gonna tell us that you're lending your gun to this cause," Guthrie said to Clint, "I'm outta here."

"What cause, Mr. Guthrie?" Clint asked. "What is the cause here?"

"Gettin' rid of the Knights of Masonry."

"Well, it doesn't sound like a cause anyone is working toward."

"So you're not gonna get rid of them for us?" the man asked.

"You think my gun can run the Knights out of Utopia?" Clint asked.

"And that's another thing," Heller said. "I want the name of the town put back to what it was—Beldon."

Clint took out his gun and they all flinched, except for the old man who was sucking the last inch of whiskey from the bottle.

"With this?" Clint asked. "Drive them out, and change the name of the town back. Is that it?"

"Yes," Guthrie said.

"No," Rita said, taking her own gun out, "with this too. Alex?"

Alex Lincoln reached down and picked up a rifle Clint hadn't seen before.

"And with this."

"There you go," Guthrie said. "You got your backup. Make it happen. Otherwise, leave us alone."

He headed for the door.

"Mark—"

"Let him go," Jake Heller said. "He's right, Alex." He followed Guthrie.

"Come back, Jake," Alex said.

The two men left the building.

"Charlie?" Alex said to the liveryman.

"What can I do, Alex?" the man asked. "I got a rifle, sure, but I can't hit nothin' with it."

"You can help me persuade other people," Alex said.

"Sure, I can do that," Charlie said. "You just get them here." He looked at Clint. "Sorry, Adams."

He started to leave, and Alex said, "Charlie, can you take Hector with you?"

"Sure." He reached for the old man, pulled him to his feet, and tossed one arm around his neck. "Come on, old-timer."

Rita went to open the door for them, then locked it and came back.

"So it's just the three of us," Rita said.

"What can we do?" Alex asked.

"I know one thing we can do," Rita said before Clint could respond.

"What's that, Rita?"

"We could burn down their meeting place," she said. "That place they call a Masonic temple."

"That's not gonna do nothin', Rita," Alex said. "They'll meet someplace else."

"It's a start."

"I gotta go upstairs to bed," Alex said. "You folks let yourselves out."

"Can we talk again, Alex?" Clint asked.

"Sure, Adams," the other man said. "We can always talk."

He left them by another door, presumably to go to a room upstairs, where he lived.

"This is what I've had to deal with for months," Rita said to Clint. "Men with no guts."

"Don't be too hard on them, Rita," Clint said. "They're right. They're all storekeepers."

"They're men," she said. "Men ought to fight for what's theirs."

"Too bad there aren't some men in town with your guts and attitude."

"Well," she said, coming closer to him, putting one hand on his chest, "at least with you in town, we got one real man here."

She put her other hand someplace else.

"Clint Adams is the Gunsmith," Zack Franklin said. "Is he in town?"

"You hadn't heard?"

"I don't talk to people," Zack said.

"But you can hear—"

"I stay away from people," Zack said. "I like whores and bartenders."

"Fine," the Grand Master said. "Yes, he is in town, and he may be a problem for us. Apparently, he doesn't approve of the Knights of Masonry."

"So what do you want me to do?" Zack asked. "Exactly."

"I want you to handle him," the Master said. "Take care of him."

"Talk plainer."

"Zack," the man behind the desk said, "I want you to kill Clint Adams."

Zack nodded. "That's plain enough."

THIRTY-FOUR

"I'm not a shy woman, Mr. Gunsmith," Rita said, pressing herself against him. "As soon as you walked in here, I knew a real man had come to town. Do you know how long it's been since I had a real man between my legs? No, you wouldn't know, but—"

He shut her up by grabbing her, pulling her close, and kissing her. The kiss went on a long time, their mouths and faces becoming slippery with it. He wrapped her long red hair around his fingers and pulled her head back so he could kiss her neck. Their breath came noisily and they started undressing each other, gun belts hitting the floor first, and then articles of clothing. In a flash they were naked, and he pushed her away because he wanted to look at her. She staggered back against some boxes and then steadied herself, glaring at him.

She was a magnificent sight, tall, full-breasted, big nipples standing at attention, too dark to be pink, too light to be brown. The thatch of hair between her legs was as red as the hair on her head, and her legs were long and graceful. She was breathing hard, her nostrils flaring, her chest heaving, and she was looking him up and down with a frank approval he rarely saw in women. She was right, there was nothing shy about her, which she proved with her next words.

"Come on, Gunsmith," she said. "Fuck me. Let's consummate our partnership."

"There's no partnership," he said, "but I'll fuck you with pleasure."

She came at him then, grabbed his cock in one hand and his balls in the other.

"No partnership?" she asked, biting his chin.

If she meant to hold his privates hostage, she changed her mind immediately. Instead, she stroked his cock and fondled his balls, then went down to her knees, avid mouth all over him. She sucked his testicles, licked the length of his penis, and then took him in her mouth. Once again, he wrapped his fingers in her beautiful hair while she bobbed up and down on him, sucking him like a woman possessed. He looked down, saw the freckles that dappled her shoulders and her gorgeous back, leaned over, and slid one hand down her back until he could run his middle finger along her butt crack. His own breath began coming in rasps as she was determined to turn him inside out with her mouth. Finally, he had to pull her off him and push her away once again, but not far. As she staggered against some boxes, knocking some over, he went after her. He lifted her up onto a box, then slid his arms beneath her thighs. Holding her that way, he entered her, and she gasped as he pierced her deeply. They were still knocking things over, and Clint wondered for a moment if Alex could hear them from upstairs.

She bounced up and down on his hard cock, clutching at him, scratching his back, sliding her hands down to dig her nails into his buttocks and pull on him so he'd fuck her harder.

He kissed her mouth, her neck, her shoulders, the slopes

of her breasts. He withdrew his penis from her and it came away glistening with her love juices. He dropped to his knees and buried his face in her wetness, breathing her scent in deeply. He licked her, loving the taste of her. He curled his tongue and poked it in and out of her, then licked the length of her slit while she gasped and grunted. At one point, when he found her hard little clit, she pushed one fist into her mouth to keep from screaming.

She became wetter and wetter, growing taut, trembling with need.

"Back," she said, grabbing at him, "come back. Get inside me. Fuck me, damn it."

He stood up and slid right into her again. She was steamy, wet, eager. She pulled at him down there like a wet, sucking mouth.

He fucked her, felt himself growing harder and longer than he could remember ever being. He felt powerful with this woman, as if he could go on all night with her, and he felt sure she felt the same way.

It had to end sometime, but not yet, he told himself. Jesus, not yet . . .

Zack Franklin could hardly contain himself.

"I can see from your face that this is a task you'd like to take on."

"I'd do this one for free," Zack said, adding quickly, "but I won't."

"No, you won't," the Grand Master said. "You'll be paid well."

"When do you want it done?"

"We are meeting Friday night to discuss delicate matters," the Grand Master said. "I'd like you to have it done by then."

The Grand Master reached into his top desk drawer and withdrew an envelope.

"Half now and half when the deed is done," he said, handing it over.

Zack accepted the envelope, enjoyed the thickness and weight of it. Holding it in his hand, he stood up.

"Consider it done."

"This is important," the Grand Master said, holding up his right index finger, as if he were going to teach a valuable lesson to a student. "I want him dead, I don't care how you do it. But please keep the needs of the many above your own needs."

"Huh?"

"The Knights of Masonry need this man out of the way," the Grand Master said. "Don't let your ego get in the way. You may go *mano a mano* with him if you like, but I hope you'll do something more . . . inventive, something . . . definite."

"I get it," Zack said. "You don't want me facin' him in the street. You want me to back shoot him. You want a sure thing."

"A sure thing," the Grand Master repeated. "Yes, that's it. I want a sure thing."

Zack tapped his envelope of money on the desk thoughtfully.

"Don't worry," he said. "It'll get done."

THIRTY-FIVE

Clint cupped Rita's ass, lifted her, and carried her across the room, even as their mouths were avidly mashed together. He settled her down on some feed bags, a lower perch than they had been using, so he was able to go down with her. Once he had her on her back, he began to pound himself in and out of her. She lifted her legs into the air for him, her breath coming hard, her firm breasts flattening only slightly. Her slick juices were wetting both of them, as well as the burlap bag beneath them. Neither of them were concerned with what the burlap must be doing to the flesh of her ass.

"Ooh, God," she said in a raspy tone. "Oh, yes, I knew it, I knew it. . . ."

He didn't know what she thought she knew, but he continued thrusting in and out of her as hard as he could, sliding his hands beneath her butt, feeling the slickness of her juices even there.

He felt every muscle in both of their bodies grow taut, and then she began to buck beneath him, crying out, reaching her climax just seconds before his came rushing out. . . .

• • •

Clint strapped on his gun belt and said, "Alex must've heard us upstairs."

"His room is on the other side of the building," she said. "Besides, I don't care. I haven't done that in a long time."

"Well, you haven't forgotten how," he told her. "You were very good."

"Good?" she said. "We were great. We're doin' that again before you leave town."

"It's a date," he said.

"As long as we're alive," she added.

He looked around, saw the boxes they'd knocked over, and the big wet spot on the burlap bag.

"I, uh, think we should straighten up here." He pointed to the wet spot. "And cover that up."

"Jesus," she said, "you made me so wet."

Just hearing her say that made his penis jump.

"Okay," he said, "more talk like that and we'll be right back at it."

"That's okay with me," she told him, starting to unbutton her shirt again.

"No, no," he said, "we have to get out of here."

"Buy me a drink and I'll help you clean up."

"Deal."

Zack Franklin left the Grand Master's house the same way he came in, shown the way to the back door by Cyrus.

"Hey, Cyrus," he said before he left.

"Yes, sir?"

"You ever read any of them books?"

"Yes, sir," the black man said. "The Master allow me free access to his library."

"You can read?" Zack asked.

"I read very well, sir."

"Anythin' in that library that would interest me?" he asked.

He did not notice the sarcasm in the black man's tone as Cyrus said, "I very much doubt that, sir."

"Yeah, me neither," Zack said. " 'Night, Cyrus."

"Good night, sir."

Clint and Rita went to The Whiskey after they finished setting the place right. Clint had moved a bunch of feed bags and put the wet one on the bottom. He didn't know what Alex's relationship was with Rita, but he didn't want to rub anything in the man's face either.

In fact, he didn't know Alex's relationship with Harriet either. He hoped he wasn't getting in the middle of anything with the storekeeper and either woman. Rita, though, didn't seem like the kind of woman who would settle.

"Whiskey," she told the bartender. It wasn't Bud Cook tonight, but another man with heavy black stubble and equally black hair on both arms. "And don't get any of your damn hair in it, Willy."

"A little of my hair would do ya some good, Red," the man said with a laugh.

"Beer," Clint said.

The man set him up and then moved down the bar.

Rita drank half her whiskey and set the glass down.

"I needed that," she said. "You about wore me out, Mr. Gunsmith."

"I told you, no more talk like that," he said, "unless you want me to throw you up onto this bar."

She put her hand on the top button of her shirt and said, "I'm ready."

The saloon was as crowded as he'd seen it during his stay. He wished he had the nerve to call her bluff.

"You're just crazy enough to do it," he said.

She laughed, picked up her whiskey, drained it, and said, "Now you're gettin' it, Mr. Gunsmith."

"Could you do me a favor, Rita?" he asked.

"Anything."

"Could you stop calling me that?"

THIRTY-SIX

Zack Franklin went into the small saloon that catered to Freemasons. He found Al Fortune standing at the bar. Fortune wasn't a Mason, but they allowed him to drink there.

"Had your big meetin'?" Fortune asked.

"Yep." He looked at the bartender. "Beer."

Silently, the bartender filled the order. Zack looked around. The place was about half filled, and quiet. There was nothing going on but drinking.

"Jesus," he said to Fortune, "Masons don't talk much, do they?"

"Got me. They let me drink here because I do jobs for the mayor. What's this big job they want you for?" Fortune asked.

"Clint Adams is in town."

"I heard."

"They want him out of town—in a box."

"Ah."

"Up to me how I do it."

"Which way you leanin'?"

"I'd really like to try 'im, you know?" Zack said, rubbing his hand over his jaw.

125

"Wouldn't mind it myself," Fortune admitted.

"But there's big money in it for me if I just get it done."

"I told Calhoun I'd charge four times my usual fee," Fortune said. "That's probably still not as much as you're gettin'."

Zack had the envelope with half his money stuffed into his back pocket.

"You askin' me how much I'm gettin'?"

"Hell, no, Zack," Fortune said. "I wouldn't ask you about your money."

There was a tense moment when Fortune knew Zack was capable of blowing up, but it passed when Zack suddenly laughed and slapped him on the back.

"Speakin' of money," he said, "what'd ya think about that little Chinee gal? She took it all, huh?"

Rita finished her whiskey and took a beer next. Clint was still working on his. He could see where Rita could make some men feel inferior to her. That was probably why the men at the meeting had had a hard time with her.

"Do you know any of the other people—men or women—" Then he stopped short. "Do you not want to talk about this out in the open?"

"I really don't give a damn who hears me complainin', Clint," she said. It was the first time she'd used his name and not called him "Mr. Gunsmith."

"Do you know other folks you can approach?" he asked. "Or is it up to Alex?"

"What made you get connected with Alex?" she asked, preferring to ask her own question rather than answer his.

"Harriet Willis put us together," he said.

"Harriet?"

"Yes, I'm staying at her hotel."

"Watch out for that one, Clint."

"Why?" he asked. "She seems really sweet."

"She's got her own agenda goin'," Rita said. "Me and her, we don't get along at all."

"Is it because you're both beautiful women?"

"Now see, I don't get that," she replied. "I've heard Alex say that too."

"Say what?"

"That Harriet Willis is beautiful. I don't see it at all."

"Well, I—"

"And she ain't as sweet as she makes out," Rita went on. "She's got every man in town bamboozled."

"Seems like you're pretty angry with her."

"Angry?" Her eyes widened, nostrils flared, but then she got herself under control.

"I just don't like 'er," she said. "That's all. Okay, look, yes, there are folks I can talk to. There's women who aren't happy. Maybe I can get them to press their men to do something."

"Well, however you can do it," he said, "if we can get some more people at another meeting, maybe we can accomplish something."

"Let me ask you somethin'," she said.

"Go ahead."

"I get that you don't want to be the leader," she said. "But will you be there with us? I mean, if it comes to gun-play, can I count on you to watch my back?"

"You can count on me to watch your back, Rita," he said, "whatever happens."

THIRTY-SEVEN

On his way back to the hotel, Clint remembered that Harriet had asked him to come back and tell her he was okay after the meeting. Instead, he'd dallied with Rita afterward, and then gone to the saloon. He wondered if she'd still be awake, and if she was, would she be angry with him? Entering the hotel—nobody behind the front desk—he felt oddly like a husband trying to sneak into his house after playing poker late into the night.

"Clint? Is that you?" Harriet's voice came from down the hall, and then she appeared behind the desk. "That was a long meeting."

"Very long," he said, "and tiring."

"Can you tell me about it?" she asked.

"Not much to tell," Clint said. "There were about six of us—although all one man did was drain a bottle of whiskey."

"That must have been Hector."

"Exactly."

"Who else was there?"

"Mmm, a fella named Heller, one named . . . Guthrie, and Charlie from the livery."

128

"That's all? You're not going to get much done with that bunch."

"You're right again."

"Anyone else?"

"There was a woman who worked for Alex," Clint said. "Her name was . . ."

"Rita," Harriet said, the distaste plain on her face. "Rita O'Doyle. A big, blowsy red-haired tramp."

"Tramp?"

"You don't know her history."

"She didn't seem very blowsy to me," Clint said.

"She's . . . mannish, always wearing that gun."

"She's supposed to be pretty good with it," Clint said. "I guess I'll have to find out how good."

"I don't see what men see in her," Harriet said. "Will you be coming to bed?"

"I'm really beat, Harriet," he said, "and I want to get up early tomorrow morning. I think I'll just go to my room."

She studied him for a long time, and he wondered if she could smell Rita on him. He started to squirm under her scrutiny, getting that husband feeling again. He didn't like it.

"Well, good night, Harriet. I'll see you in the morning."

He started up the stairs, waiting for her to say something else, but she never did. She just watched him go up.

In his room, he locked the door, jammed a chair under the doorknob, then set the pitcher and basin on the windowsill, where anyone trying to get in would knock them over.

He wished he had a way of getting in touch with Washington, but there was none. He couldn't very well use the telegraph in town, not knowing whether or not the clerk was a Mason. He'd known going in he'd be on his own. That was why they had chosen him. Because he was used to being on his own, and because of who he was.

He got into bed, thinking about Rita and Harriet, wondering why there was so much animosity there. It was his experience that when two women disliked each other so intensely, it was usually because of a man.

He wondered how Harriet was going to treat him after he rejected her offer of her bed, but he just couldn't see himself having another night with her like they'd had, not after being with Rita. He truly was beat, and all he wanted was to sleep.

Which he did.

THIRTY-EIGHT

When Clint opened his door to the early morning knock, he expected to see Harriet standing there. Instead, it was Sheriff Jim Gentile.

"You're tryin' to drum up trouble, ain't ya?" the lawman said.

"Wha—who—what the hell are you talking about?" Clint demanded. "What time is it?"

"Time for you to get dressed and meet me downstairs," Gentile said.

"I'm not finished sleeping, Sheriff."

"You're finished sleepin' in this town if you're not downstairs in fifteen minutes, Adams," Gentile said. "We gotta talk."

"About what?"

"About you tryin' to get people in this town killed," Gentile said. "Downstairs, fifteen."

The sheriff stalked off down the hallway and down to the lobby.

Clint closed the door, got dressed, and followed the man down in twelve minutes.

• • •

131

"Where are we going?" Clint asked as he followed the sheriff out of the hotel.

"My office," Gentile said. "I don't want to discuss this in public."

"We could have talked in my room," Clint said.

"Just wait until we get indoors," Sheriff Gentile said.

Clint, still not fully awake, squinted at the early morning sun and followed the lawman to his office.

"You got any coffee?" he asked as they entered.

"Pot's on the stove," Gentile said. "Pour me one too."

Clint poured two mugs full and carried them back to the sheriff. He handed the man a cup and then sat down opposite him.

He sipped his coffee and asked, "Now what's this all about?"

"You had a secret meeting last night where you tried to incite a bunch of storekeepers to pick up guns and burn down the Masonic temple."

"Whoa, whoa," Clint said. "Where are you getting this information from?"

Gentile thought about that for a moment, then said, "Mark Guthrie is my brother-in-law."

"Guthrie?"

"He told me about the meeting."

"Did he tell you I wanted to burn down the temple?" Clint asked. "That wasn't my idea."

"Whose was it then?"

"It was . . . somebody else's," Clint said as he recalled that it had been Rita who suggested that.

"Well, what about the rest?"

"I wasn't trying to incite anybody to do anything," Clint said. "I was just trying to find out where the people of this town really stand."

"They stand in fear," Gentile said, "and there's nobody here who will do anything about it."

"Isn't that your job, Sheriff?"

Gentile slammed down his mug so hard that it shattered, sending coffee all over the place.

"Don't tell me my job!" he shouted.

Clint sat still and quiet and stared at the man until Gentile, feeling foolish, sat back down, coffee dripping from his hand and staining his sleeve.

"Okay," he said. "Okay. I just want to know what's goin' on, Adams. What are you trying to do?"

Clint had told Harriet what he was doing in Utopia. Since being with Rita, and being warned, he was wondering if he'd made such a good choice. Now he was faced with another choice. Tell the local law, or not?

"Let me make this easier for you," Gentile said. "Did you know a man named Ted Lilly?" Clint hesitated. "Ted Lilly" was the alias the government man who was missing had gone by. His real name was Roscoe Bookman. Was Gentile telling him that he knew about "Lilly"?

"I don't think I ever knew a man by that name," Clint said warily.

"Okay," Gentile said, "how about Roscoe Bookman?"

"How do you know Roscoe Bookman?"

"You tellin' me you didn't know him?" the lawman asked.

"Not personally," Clint said, "but I know the name."

"Okay," Gentile said. "Bookman confided in me that he was here investigating the Knights of Masonry."

"And oddly," Clint said, "he's disappeared."

"And that makes me look bad?"

"Let's just say it could look suspicious."

"Until you find out I wasn't the only person he confided in."

"He told someone else?"

"Yes."

"Who?"

"You won't like it."

"Just tell me."

"All right," Gentile said. "He told me that he also confided in Harriet Willis."

THIRTY-NINE

Clint got up from his chair, walked to the cell block, found it empty, then went and checked the window to see if anyone was outside.

"I don't blame you for bein' suspicious," Gentile said.

"I'm just being careful."

Clint retrieved his coffee mug, refilled it, and then sat back down. He didn't ask the sheriff if he wanted another cup.

"When did Bookman confide in you?"

"After he was here a few days," Gentile said. "He said he was here with a partner."

"Who has also disappeared," Clint added.

"From here?"

"No," Clint said, "after he returned to Washington. Did you ever meet him?"

"Never met 'im, don't know what his name was," Gentile said.

"When was the last time you saw Bookman?"

"The night before he disappeared."

"And what happened the night he disappeared?" Clint asked.

"It was the night of a meeting in the temple," the lawman said. "He told me he was gonna try to get into the building and eavesdrop."

"And he disappeared."

"I'm convinced he's dead," Gentile said. "I told you already, I know these damned Knights have committed murder but I can't prove it. He was one of the ones I was talking about."

Clint stared at the lawman. He could have known who Bookman was because he was a Knight, and was in on killing him. If he was telling the truth, though, then Clint had made a huge mistake confiding in Harriet, and that meant he'd let his penis get him into a bad situation.

"You're tryin' to decide who to trust, me or Harriet," Gentile said. "Well, let me tell you, I've always trusted Harriet myself."

"What about Rita O'Doyle?"

"Rita?" Gentile asked. "She's Alex Lincoln's bull whacker. What's she got to do with any of this?"

"She warned me about Harriet Willis."

"Is that a fact?"

Of course, Gentile could have been telling Clint that he trusted Harriet because they were both members of the Knights.

"Wait," Clint said. "Women aren't allowed to be Masons, are they? Or Knights?"

"No, it's a boys' club."

Then what would Harriet have to gain by turning Bookman in to the Knights? With each thought, Clint was making a case to trust Harriet, then Gentile, then neither, and then both.

He was going to have to go with his gut. It would have been nice to be able to send a telegram and check Gentile out with some other lawmen Clint knew, but that wasn't going to happen.

Unless . . .

"What's the nearest town?"

"Ellerton," Gentile said. "It's about thirty miles. Happens to be the county seat—which is something else the Knights want to change."

"If the Knights succeed in making Utopia the county seat . . ."

"Then they broaden the area of their influence," the lawman said. "I know."

"Is there a telegraph office in Ellerton?"

"Yep," Gentile said. "But we have one here."

"And are the clerks at the telegraph office here Masons?"

"That I don't know."

"Well, there's less chance that they're Masons if I go to Ellerton, right?"

"Why do you want to send telegrams—oh, wait. You want to check me out."

"I have a few things I'd like to check out."

"Well, there's no guarantee the Masons don't already have some people there."

"Who's the law there?"

"Gary Hastings," Gentile said. "Been a lawman thirty years, been there for ten."

"What are the chances he's a Mason? Or a Knight? Or whatever we're supposed to call them?"

"Next to none," Gentile said. "Gary's a devout Catholic, his wife even more."

"Are there still churches in Ellerton?"

"Oh, yeah, two."

It was sounding more and more like Clint should go to Ellerton.

"If you head there," Gentile said, "you're gonna make a target out of yourself on the road. Easy pickin's for a bushwhacker."

"Might be a chance I have to take."

"I'd go with you, but . . ."

"I know, you have no deputies."

"Maybe there's somebody in town you can think of to take with you to watch your back."

"What about Al Fortune?"

"He's a good man with a gun, but he works for the mayor," Gentile said. "I'd never trust him. And if somebody tries to bushwhack you, it might be him on the other end of the rifle."

Clint gave it some thought.

"Does the sheriff in Ellerton have deputies?"

"Yeah, two."

"What if he loaned you one?"

"I've already talked to Gary," Gentile said. "He's determined to keep the Masons out of Ellerton. That means he can't leave there and come here to help. I'm sure that goes for his deputies too."

"Well . . ."

"Don't tell me," Gentile said. "Don't tell me what you decide, and don't tell me who you find to watch your back. Maybe you'll come back from Ellerton able to trust me."

It was a good point.

"Okay, Sheriff."

"But while you're there sending telegrams . . ."

"Yeah?"

"You might want to check out a few more people."

"I already had that in mind."

FORTY

"You want me to what?" Rita asked.

"Take a ride with me to Ellerton."

"What for?"

"I need to send some telegrams."

"To who?"

"I can't tell you."

"About what?"

"Can't tell you that either."

"Does it have to do with—"

"Yes."

They were in front of Alex Lincoln's feed store, and he'd found Rita loading bags of feed onto a wagon. He wondered if the bag they had wet was included.

"I'd have to get the time off from Alex."

"I think that can be arranged."

"There's nobody else in town you can ask?" she said. "Wait a minute. What am I thinking?"

"Exactly," he said. "You're the only one I feel I can trust."

"Well . . . I guess that's flattering," she said. "What's my part in this?"

"Keeping me alive."

She leaned against the wagon, removed her hat to wipe sweat from her brow. She had soaked through under the arms of the man's shirt she was wearing. Her skin glistened with perspiration. She looked amazingly sexy.

"There's a really good steak house in Ellerton," she said. "Will you buy me a meal?"

"Yes."

"Stay in the best hotel in town?"

"Definitely."

She put her hat back on.

"When do we leave?"

"Tomorrow morning. I want to get back in time for the Masons' meeting Friday night."

"You're going to their meeting?"

"Maybe," he said, "but they don't know it yet. So what about it?"

"Let me go and talk to Alex," she said. "He's just inside."

"Do you want me to come?"

"No," she said, "I can pretty well get my way with him. This won't be a tough sell."

"I'll load some of these bags for you while you're talking to him."

She touched his face and said, "I was hoping you'd say that."

Clint went back to the hotel and found Fred Anderson at the front desk.

"Hey, Fred," Clint said. "How are you today?"

"Hello, Mr. Adams," he said. "I'm, uh, fine. How are you?"

"Good," Clint said. "I'm good. Is Harriet around?"

"I think she went out to do some shopping," he said. "Is there anything I can do?"

Clint had not yet decided whether or not to tell Harriet he was leaving in the morning and would be back by Friday, but he certainly was not about to tell Fred. That was one way to make sure the news got back to the mayor.

"No," Clint said. "I'll just talk to her later."

As he turned to go up the stairs, Rita appeared at the front door.

"Good news," she said, but he cut her off with a wave. He grabbed her arm and they went outside.

"Not in front of him."

"Oh, okay. Anyway, Alex is fine with me bein' gone overnight—for one day. He's got a busy weekend comin' up."

"Okay," Clint said. "We'll leave first thing in the morning. Should be about a five-hour ride, unless we push it."

"I got a good horse," she said, "and I know you got a good horse. I think we can make it in three hours."

"Let's split the difference and do it in four," he said.

"Fine with me," she said. "I'm gonna go and clean my rifle."

"And your revolver."

She touched it and said, "I always keep that clean."

"Show me."

She took the gun from her holster and handed it over. It was a Peacemaker, which would be too big and unwieldy for most women. He checked the action, the weight, even found a fresh smudge of oil. She was right, she did keep it clean.

"Good," he said, handing it back.

"Anythin' else we gonna need?" she asked.

"Nope," he said. "We'll be riding there and back with no other stops. In fact, we might even be able to make it back the same day."

"Oh, no," she said. "Dinner and a hotel. You promised."

"Okay," he said. "Dinner and a hotel."

She started away, then stopped and turned back.

"Who else knows we're goin'?"

"Nobody for sure."

"But?"

"The sheriff knows that I might go," he said. "He doesn't know when, and he doesn't know who will be going with me."

"So if we get bushwhacked, we can trace it back to him?" she asked.

"Maybe," he said. "Unless I'm being watched all the time."

"Ain't that something a man with your rep would know?" she asked.

"Usually," he said.

"Okay," she said. "Should we meet in front of the livery?"

"Yep," he said. "First light."

"I'll be there," she said. "Don't go gettin' killed today. I'll be real mad if I don't get my steak and hotel room."

"I'll keep that in mind," he promised.

FORTY-ONE

Clint went to the livery to check on Eclipse. He found Charlie tending to the horse.

"How's he doing, Charlie?" he asked.

"He's doin' real good, Clint," Charlie said. "I'm just makin' sure he's happy. You takin' him out?"

"Not today," Clint said, "but I thought I'd take him for a run tomorrow morning."

"First thing?"

"Yeah, pretty early."

"I'll have him ready."

"Hey, Charlie," Clint said, "tell me something about this fella Paul Wayne."

"He's a big shot," Charlie said. "Lots of money he made up north."

"Any idea how he made it?"

"I've heard people say shippin', some say bankin'," Charlie answered. "Heard others say whores. Coulda been all three."

"Where does he live?"

"Good part of town, big brick house," Charlie said.

143

"Only comes to town every so often to tell us how much better he is than we are."

"Charlie . . . could he be the Grand Master?" Clint asked.

"What would make you say that?"

"I haven't heard a thing about him since I came to town, except to see him with you," Clint said. "Nobody ever mentions him. Seems to me that's the kind of person who would be the Grand Master."

"Except for one thing."

"What's that?"

"He hates bein' around people," Charlie said.

"You just told me he comes to town to give people a hard time."

"Yeah, one at a time," Charlie said. "It was me last time. Next time it will be somebody else. If he's Grand Master, he's got to go to those meetings and be in a room full of people."

"So you don't think it's him?"

"No."

"Do you have a guess about who it could be?"

"No."

"Why not?"

"Because it ain't healthy."

"Charlie—"

"It ain't even healthy to talk to you about it, Clint. I'll have your horse ready for you at first light."

"Talk to me about something else then," Clint said. "About somebody else."

"Like who?"

"The sheriff," Clint said. "And Harriet Willis."

"What about them?"

"Which one of them would you trust?"

"With what?"

"Your life."

"That's easy," Charlie said. "The sheriff."

"Why him?"

"Because he can use a gun."

"Okay," Clint said, "let me phrase it a different way. You have something you want to tell someone, but if they pass it on it'll get you killed. Which one of them would you tell?"

"Neither one."

"Who in town would you tell?"

"You."

"Me? Why me?"

"Because you're the Gunsmith," Charlie said. "Because you're new in town."

"Charlie—"

"Okay, okay," Charlie said, "you're tryin' ta get me to tell you who I trust in town. Who I don't think is connected to the Knights."

"Yes."

"Okay, that's easy. I'd tell a woman, any woman."

"Because women aren't allowed to join."

"Right."

Clint sighed. He wasn't going to get the help he wanted— the answers he wanted—out of Charlie. The man was too careful about what he said, even to a stranger in town.

"Okay, Charlie," he said. "Thanks."

He left the livery and went to The Whiskey for a drink.

When he walked in, he saw Al Fortune at the bar finishing a beer.

"You want another one, Al?" he asked.

"I always want another one, Adams."

Clint held up two fingers to the bartender, Bud Cook, and pointed to Fortune's beer.

"What's the occasion?" Fortune asked.

"You're here, I'm here," Clint said. "Does there have to be an occasion to drink beer?"

"Not for me."

Cook set two beers down and they each picked one up.

"This is a real quiet town," Clint said.

"Ain't that the way folks like their towns?" Fortune asked. "Quiet."

"Yeah, but these people are quiet because they're scared."

"I ain't scared."

"You can take care of yourself."

"Every man should be able to take care of himself," Fortune said. "If he can't, he ain't a man."

"You think any of these storekeepers in town should be able to step out into the street and face, oh, say . . . you? And hold their own with a gun?"

"They should be ready to die with a gun in their hand, defending themselves and what's theirs."

"Well, I guess if that was the case, then the Knights of Misery wouldn't have such a stranglehold on the town, would they?"

"I guess not."

Clint waited a beat and then asked, "Aren't you going to tell me not to say that?"

"Say what?"

"Knights of Misery."

Fortune shrugged. "What do I care what you call 'em?"

"Well, everyone else in town gets nervous when I use that term."

"I ain't the nervous type."

Clint thought that if Fortune were someone he could trust, he would have been ideal to take with him to Ellerton. But he couldn't trust him.

"Hey, Al, is there anybody in this town that you are absolutely sure is not a member of the Knights?"

"Yeah."

"Who?"

"First me," Fortune said, "and then you."

"And that's it?"

"That's it."

"And that doesn't make you nervous?"

"No," Al Fortune said, "all it makes me is careful."

FORTY-TWO

In spite of the situation, Clint found himself liking Al Fortune. There was no pretense about the man. He wasn't a member of the Knights of Misery. He'd drink with Clint all day and then kill him that night if somebody paid him. You couldn't find anybody more honest than that.

"I was you," Fortune said to Clint over a second beer, "I'd leave this town fast."

"Is that a warning, Al?" Clint asked. "You warning me off to keep me safe?"

Fortune shrugged. "I'm just sayin', is all."

"Who do I have to be careful of?"

"Ain't you been listenin'?" Fortune asked him. "Everybody!"

"Nobody in particular?"

Fortune finished his beer and said to Clint, "I ain't got nothin' more to say on the subject."

"Well, I appreciate what you did say, Al," Clint said. "Thanks."

"Don't thank me," Fortune said on his way out. "I ain't done you no favors."

•   •   •

On the street, Al Fortune wondered what the hell he was doing. He didn't even know Adams and he was warning him. Where had that come from? There was no profit in warning the Gunsmith that Zack Franklin was coming after him, and Al Fortune rarely did anything that wasn't for profit.

He knew Franklin better than he knew Adams. Why make it harder for Zack? Then again, he was really interested to see who came out on top, Zack or Adams—but that was in a fair fight. He found that he didn't take to the idea of Zack shooting Adams in the back. That was no way for a man with a reputation like that to die. Look at Hickok. All the things he had done in his life, he was best known for being shot in the back and killed by a coward.

Getting shot in the back by a gunman as good as Zack Franklin was no better.

He shook his head and walked down the street. What the hell, he'd finally found a man he thought he could like as a friend.

Was that so bad?

"He's right, you know," Bud Cook said, putting another beer in front of Clint. "On the house."

"Thanks." Clint picked it up. "Right about what? Not doing me any favors?"

"That, but also about leavin' town. You'd be better off."

"Why's that?"

"Because I can see what you're doin'."

"And what's that?"

"You're thinkin' you're gonna save this town," Cook said, "but you ain't."

"Why not?"

"Because one man can't do it," Cook said, "and that's all you are, one man. You ain't gonna get any help in this town."

"What about you, Bud?"

"Me?"

"Yeah," Clint said. "You're a good bartender. That means you got a shotgun under the bar. Every good bartender does. And that probably means you know how to use it. So how about it? You want to help me save this town?"

"It ain't a two-man job either," Cook said. "And I ain't crazy."

"What if I told you there'd be more than two men?" Clint asked. "What if I told you there'd be enough men—enough people—to pull it off?"

Bud Cook backed away from the bar until be bumped into the bottles behind him.

"You're talkin' about a war," he said. "About bodies in the streets by the time it's done."

Clint stared at the man, then laughed and said, "No, I'm not, Bud. I'm just talking, is all." He drank down half the fresh beer and put the mug back on the counter. "Thanks for the drink."

He walked out without another word.

Zack Franklin watched from across the street as Clint Adams left The Whiskey Saloon. Earlier, he'd watched Al Fortune come out. Coincidence. It never occurred to him that Al might have told Adams about him.

He watched as the Gunsmith stepped into the street and started across. Nobody was on the street. It was as if the people in town knew that trouble was brewing. Zack could have stepped out and done it right there and then, faced down the Gunsmith, shot him down in the street. Made his money, and his rep.

He could've.

He didn't.

Clint noticed the quiet—the silence—on the street as he stepped out. Something was in the air and the townspeople knew it. They were in their homes, or their shops, but the point was they were behind closed and locked doors, peering out their windows, waiting.

They were waiting for something to happen, but it wasn't going to happen today. Clint had learned long ago to count on his instincts, and they were telling him, "Not today!"

He walked across the street, prepared—despite what his instincts told him—for trouble. A shot from above, a challenge on the street.

Never came.

Chalk up one more for his instincts. Problem was, his instincts also told him it was coming soon . . . very, very soon.

He knew he could count on that too.

FORTY-THREE

Clint managed to go to bed that night without seeing Harriet. Early the next morning, however, she was behind the desk when he came down.

"You're up early," she said without a smile.

"I, uh, have something to do."

"I see." She was glaring at him. The sweet Harriet from a couple of days ago was gone. More and more he was thinking that he'd confided in the wrong person. Not only because she might be connected to the Knights, but because she was a woman. Even if she wasn't connected, she might consider herself a woman scorned, and there was never any telling what such women would do.

"Harriet—"

"You don't have to explain anything to me, Clint," she said. "And you don't have to worry about me talking about why you're here. You just go and do what you've got to do . . . with whoever you think you have to do it with."

He thought about giving her an explanation, but decided he didn't want to keep Rita waiting at the livery.

"I'll see you," he said, and left the hotel.

•   •   •

At the livery he found Rita waiting with her horse saddled, and Charlie waiting with Eclipse ready to go.

"He's lookin' ta run," Charlie said, handing Clint the reins.

"Charlie, we might be back late."

"That's fine."

"Or even tomorrow."

Charlie looked out at Rita, tall and stately in her boots, pants, and shirt. The shirt was big on her, but did nothing to hide her proud breasts, and the pants fit her just right, hugging the cheeks of her ass. She was a helluva sight.

"Hey," Charlie said, "you go ahead and do what you gotta do, huh?"

"See you, Charlie."

"He walked Eclipse out to where Rita was standing with her mount, a powerful-looking six-year-old mare.

"That's an amazing-lookin' animal," she said, admiring Eclipse.

"Yes, he is."

"I hope my Lucy can stay with him."

"Lucy?"

"Hey, it's my horse, I'll name her what I want."

"Hey, okay, fine, she's Lucy."

They both mounted up, Clint sitting higher than Rita because Eclipse was much bigger than Lucy.

"We'll take it easy on your girl," he promised her.

"Hey, don't worry about us," Rita said. "We'll pull our own weight."

"I know you will," Clint said. "Let's get going."

Zack Franklin watched as Clint Adams and the red-haired woman mounted their horses and rode out of town. The woman was wearing a gun like she knew how to use it, and why else would the Gunsmith be taking her? He obviously

saw the need for someone to watch his back, and out of
everyone in town he'd chosen her.

Franklin, given the same choice, would have chosen Al
Fortune, but there were obvious reasons for Adams not to
do that.

As they rode out, Franklin was mulling things over in
his mind. Follow, ride up ahead, and wait . . . or let them go
and wait for them to return?

And were they going to return?

He decided to ask that question of the liveryman.

Clint and Eclipse set a brisk pace, not wanting to outrun the
mare, but wanting to test her a little. She kept pace for the
first hour, and then started to drop back, so Clint eased up
on the big gelding and let him trot. Since they were going
to stay in Ellerton overnight anyway, there was no point in
pushing it.

When nobody tried to ambush them the first hour, Clint
started to wonder if he was being paranoid. When he
thought about Roscoe Bookman, though, he decided not.
The Secret Service agent was gone, almost certainly dead,
as was his partner. That was not paranoia, that was fact.
According to Sheriff Gentile, other people had been killed
as well. There was still time for someone to take a shot at
him, or it could even come during the ride back.

He knew Rita would die first—and ride her horse into
the ground—before she asked for a rest, so when he
thought they were halfway there, he halted their progress.

"Let's take a breather," he said, dismounting.

"Whatever you say."

There was a road from Utopia to Ellerton, so he had decided to stick to it. They walked their horses off to the side
of the road and he picked out a rock to sit on. Rita chose
to remain standing.

She saw him watching her rub her ass and said, "I do

most of my traveling lately on a buckboard. Haven't sat a horse in a while."

"You'll get your seat back," he told her.

She looked out over the Virginia terrain, still massaging her butt. She also stretched her back, which caused her breasts to jut out. The land was hilly, with plenty of places to take cover. Clint had to pull his eyes from her hills.

"Could be somebody out there with a rifle right now," she said.

"If you see anyone, give a holler," he said. "Watch for the sun reflecting off something metal."

"Right."

"So tell me," Clint said, just to make conversation while he also swept the terrain with his eyes, "what's between you and Alex?"

She looked at him sharply.

"What? Me and Alex? Nothin', why?"

"Hey, you're a woman, he's a man, you work together. . . ."

"You're a man, Clint," she said. "Ain't no other men in that town, except maybe Al Fortune and that crazy man, Zack Franklin."

"Why is he crazy?"

"Because he likes to hurt people," she said. "He likes it a lot."

"For money?"

"Men for money," she said. "Women for fun."

"Does he kill for money?"

"I'd put money on it."

"And Fortune?"

"Him too," she agreed, "but he don't enjoy it like Franklin does."

"Do you know either of them well?"

She looked at him and smiled lasciviously.

"Not as well as I know you."

Zack Franklin. That was a name he was going to have to keep in mind.

"You ready?" he asked.

"Ready as I'll ever be," she said. "Don't think I don't know you been takin' it easy on Lucy."

"Hey," he said, mounting up, "we'll get there when we get there."

FORTY-FOUR

They rode into Ellerton five hours after they left Utopia, so it was still before noon. He was now sorry for the promises he had made Rita about the steak and the hotel. On the other hand, there was no guarantee he'd get answers to all his telegrams on the same day. They rode to the livery stable to put their horses up for the night.

"We'll probably be leaving early tomorrow," Clint said.

"Sorry to hear it," the man said. "Ain't ever had an animal this fine in my stable."

"Just make sure he's this fine when I pick him up tomorrow," Clint said. Then he added, "Both of them."

"Don't worry," he said, "I'll take good care of them both."

"What's the best hotel in town?" Clint asked.

"That's easy. The Ellerton House."

"That figures," Clint said. "Shows a lot of imagination."

"Huh?" the man said.

"Never mind," Clint said. "Thanks."

They collected their saddlebags and rifles and left the stable.

• • •

They registered at the hotel first. It was classier than anything in Utopia, with a large lobby filled with overstuffed
chairs and tables with flowers on them.

"We better get two rooms," Clint said.

"You worried about your reputation or mine?" she
asked.

"I'm being careful," he said. "We'll both stay in the
room that you sign for."

"Oh, I see," she said. "Very smart."

"Thank you."

He got himself a room and one "for the lady," as the
clerk put it. They went up, stowed all their gear in Rita's
room.

"Wow," she said, sitting on the mattress and looking at
the overstuffed chair near the window. "This is a fancy
room."

Clint, who had been to hotels in New York and San
Francisco, said, "Yep, it's nice."

They left the hotel to go and find the telegraph office.

"How about a beer?" she asked.

"After the telegraph office," he said. "The saloons will
be open then, and we can wait there."

"And don't forget my steak."

"That's for supper," he said. "Let's think of first things
first."

They got directions from the desk clerk for the telegraph
office. Clint stationed Rita at the door outside and went in
to write out his telegrams.

He was sending three, and had composed them in his
mind during the trip. The first went to Washington, D.C.,
the second to his private detective friend Talbot Roper
in Denver, and the third to his friend Rick Hartman in
Labyrinth, Texas. The telegrams to Roper and Hartman

were virtually the same. Either man would probably be able to come up with the answers for him. The telegram to Washington, D.C., could only be answered by them.

When he came out, Rita said, "I don't see anybody payin' any attention to us."

Two men passed by and looked Rita up and down with obvious admiration.

"Well," Clint said, "not to me anyway."

FORTY-FIVE

"Saloon now?" she asked.

"Sheriff's office first."

"I'm thirsty."

"You can go to the saloon," he said. "I'll meet you there."

"Oh, no," she said. "I'm not havin' you catch a bullet while I'm havin' a beer."

"Okay," he said. "I just want to check in with the local law here, and then we'll have a cold beer."

"I'm countin' the minutes."

Sheriff Gary Hastings was coming downstairs from the second level of his brand-new brick jailhouse, where the jail cells were, when the door opened and Clint and Rita walked in. His eyes naturally went to Rita and her red hair first, but he quickly realized it was the man who should command his attention.

"Morning, Sheriff," Clint said.

"Afternoon now," the man said, reaching the main floor. "What can I do for you folks?"

He was in his fifties, a big, hard belly straining the gun

belt around his waist. The top of his head was bald, with wisps of gray hair all around it. "Ma'am," he said politely.

"Sheriff."

"This is Rita O'Doyle, Sheriff," Clint said. "She's from Utopia."

"And who would you be?"

"I was getting to that," Clint said with a smile. "My name's Clint Adams."

"What's the Gunsmith want in Ellerton?" the man asked immediately.

"That's what I'm here to tell you," Clint said. "Can we have a few minutes of your time?"

"Why not?" The man smiled at Rita. "Ain't had a pretty lady in here in a month of Sundays—let alone one wearin' a gun."

Rita gave him a wider smile.

"Have a seat, folks," he said, heading for his desk, "and tell me what's on your mind."

Clint was truthful with the sheriff. He had to trust somebody who was wearing a badge. He'd already taken a chance on Sheriff Gentile. What did Sheriff Hastings have to gain by throwing in with the Knights?

When Clint was done, the sheriff said, "I'm aware of the situation in Beldon, Mr. Adams."

"Beldon?"

"We don't recognize the new name," the man said. "And the State of Virginia hasn't recognized it either."

"I didn't know that."

"We've taken steps to make sure the Masons can't get a toehold in Ellerton, but I've got to be here to see that doesn't happen."

"You have no Masons in your town?"

"None."

"How can you be so sure?"

"I know everybody in this town," Hastings said. "And I check out every stranger who decides they're gonna stay. Believe me, the Knights of Misery are not getting in here while I'm the law—but I can't help Sheriff Gentile with his town. He's gonna have to do that himself."

"Kind of hard when he has no deputies," Rita said.

"Apparently he has you two to help him," Hastings said, and then he looked at Clint and added, "Can't you call in federal assistance?"

"As soon as I have enough evidence to warrant it," Clint said. "The government can't come barging in without good cause."

"What about if Sheriff Gentile asks for help?" Hastings asked.

"Can he do that without the okay of the mayor and the town council?" Clint asked.

"Not if Beldon is run the way we run things here," Hastings said.

"Then that's not going to happen," Clint said. "The mayor is a Mason."

"So what do you plan to do, Mr. Adams?"

"I'm working on some ideas, Sheriff," Clint said, "but I'm having a hard time finding somebody I can trust totally."

"That's why we're not even letting the Masons get a toe in here," Hastings said. "I know who I can trust in this town, and I'm keepin' it that way."

Clint moved forward and put his hand out.

"Thanks for your time, Sheriff."

They shook hands, and the sheriff nodded to Rita and said, "Ma'am." He looked at Clint. "I wish you luck."

"Thanks," Clint said. "I'll need it."

FORTY-SIX

Clint took Rita to the nearest saloon and they both had a cold beer to wash the dust from their throats.

"Ah, I needed that," she said, downing half of it. "What do we do now?"

"We need to wait for replies to the telegrams I sent out," he said. He looked around them. The saloon was small, and was doing a brisk business even this early in the day. "We could wait here, I guess."

"That's a waste of a good hotel room," she pointed out.

"True."

"And the hotel has bathtubs," she said. "We could both use a bath."

"Even more true."

"So what do you say?" she asked. "The hotel, and a bathtub?"

"Sounds good to me," he said. "Let's finish these and get to it."

They put in an order for two hot baths, and the hotel arranged for a blanket to be hanging between them to provide "the lady" with some privacy.

But the blanket was no barrier. Clint stripped down and slipped into his tub, the slightly larger of the two. He heard Rita get into her own tub and groan as the hot water soaked into her bones.

"This is Heaven," she said.

"Sure is."

"And as soon as I'm clean," she said, "it's gonna be even better."

"Better than Heaven?" he asked.

"Just wait and see."

He sat back in his tub to wait, closed his eyes, his gun hanging on a chair within easy reach. . . .

Outside the hotel, Richie Lane told his partner, Matt Howard, "I'm tellin' you, it was him. I saw him in this saloon, and he went into the Ellerton House with a red-haired woman."

"Wonder what he's gonna do in the hotel," Howard said.

"That ain't the point," Lane said. "It's the goddamn Gunsmith, Matty."

"So?"

Howard was more interested in his beer than in the Gunsmith.

"We can make a big name for ourselves by killin' the Gunsmith."

Howard frowned.

"Are you listenin'?" his partner demanded.

"Yeah, yeah, I'm listenin'," Matt Howard said, "but he's fast, Richie. Real fast."

"That's why we ain't gonna do it face-to-face, ya idiot," Lane said. "We get 'im while his goddamn pants are down."

"Pants . . . oh, you mean, him and the gal?" Howard asked.

"Why else would they be goin' into the hotel this early in the day?" Lane demanded. "Are ya with me?"

"Can we finish our beer first?" Howard asked.

"Finish your beer, Matty," Lane said. "Then we'll go over and see what the Gunsmith is doin'."

FORTY-SEVEN

Rita pushed the blanket aside and posed for Clint. Long, lean—except for her surprisingly full breasts—and clean.

"And now," she said, "more than Heaven."

She started for his tub, then reached behind her for her gun belt. She set it on the chair by his.

"His and hers," she said.

She lifted one long leg and stepped into the tub, followed with the other, and then lowered her butt until she was sitting opposite him.

"It's dirty water," he warned her.

"The same dirt that came off of me," she said. She reached under the water for him and grasped him. He reacted immediately and began to swell in her hand.

"I have an idea," he said. "Let's take this to a bed rather than a tepid bath."

She studied him for a moment, then said, "That sounds good."

She stood up and stepped from the bath. At the same moment, the door to the room was kicked open and two men with guns entered.

● ● ●

"They're takin' baths," Richie Lane told his partner, Matt Howard.

"So we wait until they're done?"

"No, Matty," Lane said. "Goddamn it, why are you so dumb? This is perfect. They're in a bathtub full of water. We walk in and fire away. End of the Gunsmith."

Matt Howard frowned. "Won't that damage the tubs?"

Exasperated, Lane said, "Take your gun out and follow me."

As the two men entered the room, the first thing they saw was a naked Rita, big breasts glistening, water dripping from her red bush. They were momentarily stunned . . . just long enough.

Clint reached out and grabbed his gun as Rita reached down and plucked hers from her holster. By the time the two gunmen recovered and tried to fire, Clint and Rita had already done so. A hail of lead drove both men out into the hall . . . where they slid down the wall to the floor.

"Crap," Clint said, stepping from the tub. He went out into the hall naked to check the two men, found them both dead.

"Put your clothes on, Rita," he said. "The sheriff should be here any minute."

"I knew this would happen," Sheriff Hastings said.

"Sheriff," Rita said, "we were just takin' baths. Clint had no way—"

"No," Hastings said as a group of men removed the two dead bodies. "I mean those idiots. I knew they'd get themselves killed sooner or later. They must have recognized you in the saloon. I'm just sorry you had to be the one to do it."

"So . . . you don't blame us?" Rita asked.

"Not at all," Hastings said. "I'm sorry your . . . baths got interrupted."

"That's . . . okay," Clint said. He was surprised at the lawman's attitude. Usually when he defended himself, the law put the blame on him for having the rep that attracted trouble.

Hastings left, and Clint and Rita were alone in the hall.

"Are we still going to our room?" she asked.

"Oh, hell, yes," he said.

FORTY-EIGHT

When they got back to the room—the one they'd taken in Rita's name—they took extra precautions anyway. As he did back in Utopia, Clint jammed a chair beneath the doorknob and then piled a pitcher and basin on the windowsill. When he turned to look at Rita, she had already removed all her clothes.

"It's no wonder those two froze," he said. "They may have been idiots, but they knew a beautiful woman when they saw one."

"And now that we won't be interrupted again," she said, "there's the little matter of a trip to Heaven and beyond that I promised you."

"And after that," he said, "that big thick steak I promised *you.*"

"Yes," she said, putting her arms out to him, "but first things first."

He quickly divested himself of all his clothes and, naked, moved toward her, his erect penis leading the way. She accepted it as if it were an offering, cradling it in both hands, then gripping it and pulling him down onto the bed with it.

"I can't wait," she said into his ear. "No playin' today."

She pulled and tugged at his penis until it was pressed to her wet vagina, and then he did the rest of the work. He pushed into her and began taking her in long, easy strokes at first. She got into the rhythm of it with him, and they moved together that way for a long time. Then, gradually, they began to pick up speed together. Soon, they were grunting with the effort as they drove against each other, and then suddenly she cried out in his ear, "I wanna be on top!"

He stopped, didn't bother to disengage. He grabbed hold of her and rolled over without losing contact with her. When she was on top, she began to ride him. She had an amazing butt, because every time she moved on him, it not only felt like he was going in and out of her, but her butt cheeks were closing on him, grabbing his penis, adding to the friction.

After the shooting, they both needed this affirmation that they were still alive, that even though they had come close to dying, here they were, enjoying each other, giving and taking pleasure. If Rita had not been naked at the very moment those men broke in, water glistening on her body, they might be dead.

Instead, they were filling the room with the sounds and smells of sex. Grunting, groaning, flesh against flesh, the wet slurp as he drove in and out of her, the smell of her juices commingling with the scent of their sweat. It was about sex, but it was also all about life.

They continued to enjoy each other until both their bodies began to tremble with the urge to release. It happened for her first and she began to buck on him, grind on him, and then he went over the edge and began to fill her up with liquid fire. . . .

"Jesus," she said, still gasping for air moments later.

"I know."

"Does that happen to you after every shooting?" she asked.

"No," he said, "only because you were here."

But if the sex was that good because it had come after a shooting, what had he been missing all these years? In the future, every time he was forced to kill some idiot who wanted to make a reputation, maybe he'd go looking for a woman afterward.

There was a knock at the door that, had it come moments ago, they might not have heard.

She grabbed the sheet and covered herself. He pulled on his trousers and grabbed his gun. Barefoot, he went to the door just as the knock was repeated.

"Who is it?"

"Telegram," a voice said.

"Slide it under the door and wait," Clint said, standing to the side in case someone fired through the door.

"Yes, sir."

If it was a trap, there would be no telegram, but immediately he saw the tallow slip of paper come sliding under the door. He picked it up, saw it was from Rick Hartman, and then opened the door. The telegraph clerk standing there was startled and stepped back.

"Sorry," Clint said. "Can't be too careful. No reply on the other two?"

"Not yet, sir."

"Okay, when they come in, bring them here. If we're not here, slide the reply under the door, okay? Don't leave it with the desk clerk. Understand?" He handed the clerk a dollar.

"Yes, sir!" the clerk said, and left.

Clint closed the door and went back to the bed. He sat down, holstered the gun, and unfolded the telegram.

"Who's that from?" she asked.

"A friend."

Rather than try to look over his shoulder at the contents of the telegram, she remained on her back with the sheet pulled up to her neck.

"Who is it about?"

"You," he said. "You'll be glad to know you're not wanted for anything."

Rick Hartman had never heard of Rita, but he'd checked her out and she had come up clean. Her description matched that of a red-haired female bounty hunter both Clint and Rick knew, but that was all.

"Well," she said, "you must be glad you haven't been in bed with a wanted felon."

He reached back and put his hand on her thigh. He could feel the warmth of her skin beneath the sheet.

"You know what?"

'What?"

"It wouldn't have mattered."

FORTY-NINE

The telegram also said that Rick had never heard of either Sheriff Gentile or Sheriff Hastings. He had nothing on an Al Fortune, but apparently Zack Franklin was known as a cold, amoral killer in several states.

"That's a lot of information for one telegram," Rita said to Clint from across the table.

They were sitting at a table in the restaurant Rita had heard of but never been to, Tucker's Steak House. The steaks were, as advertised, tasty and perfectly prepared.

"Rick's got a lot of contacts all over the country," Clint said. "I knew he'd be the first one to get back to me."

"What does he do?"

"He runs a gambling hall in Labyrinth, Texas, but before that he gambled all over the country."

"What about the other telegrams?" she asked.

"I expect Talbot Roper to answer me fairly soon from Denver, if he's in town."

"And what does he do?"

"He's the finest private detective in the country," Clint said.

"Better than Pinkerton?"

"He used to work for Pinkerton, and then he went out on his own. Yes, he's better than any Pinkerton, and that includes Allan himself."

"You talk like you know Allan Pinkerton."

"We've crossed paths once or twice."

"You must lead such an interesting life," she said, "friends with all these interesting people."

"You're right," Clint said. "My life is interesting. These past few days are a case in point. The town of Utopia is very interesting, and getting the people out from under the thumb of the Knights of Misery is interesting as well."

"I'll say," she said. "I can't wait to see how you pull that off."

"All I have to do," he said, "is get something solid to send back to Washington."

"And when you get it," she said, "you have to get out alive."

"Exactly my plan."

"But how do you plan to do it?"

"No, you don't understand," he said. "I plan to get out alive, but I don't have a plan on how to do it."

"Then . . ."

"I'll just take it as it goes, Rita."

They finished their steaks and ordered pie for dessert—apple for her, peach for him—and a pot of coffee. She seemed to like it strong, the way he did.

"You know," he said, "I was impressed with you in the bath."

"Really?" she said. "We weren't in the tub very long."

He laughed.

"I meant the way you handled yourself with your gun," he said. "I might not have gotten both of them by myself."

"Hogwash," she said. "You would have planted both of them with no problem—but thanks. I can hold my own with a gun. I told you that when we first met."

"Yes, you did. Can I ask you something personal?"

"After what we just finished doing in our room? You can ask me anything personal."

"Why do you stay? I mean if you don't like the Knights, why do you stay?"

"Honestly?"

"That's the kind of answer I prefer."

"It'll make me sound terrible."

"I won't think badly of you."

"They don't bother me."

"The Knights?"

She nodded. "I may not like what they've done in town—closing the churches, taking over businesses, putting their own mayor in—but I never went to church, I don't own a business, and I'm not a politician. See what I mean? They really don't affect my life."

"Then why would you go against them?"

"Well, I wouldn't," she said. "Not alone. I would, though, if you do, and you get some other men to. When it comes right down to it, the town would be better off without them, but whether they're there or not, my life will probably stay the same."

"I see."

"Don't get me wrong," she added. "I don't want to stay in Beldon—Utopia, whatever—forever. I'll leave soon enough. In fact, meeting you has given me the itch to just get on a horse and go."

He didn't say anything to that, and she laughed.

"Don't worry, Mr. Gunsmith," she said. "I'm not gonna ask you to take me with you."

"I never thought that."

"Yeah, right," she said. "You should've seen the look on your face."

She continued to tease him about it all through dessert.

FIFTY

After supper they took a walk around town, though Rita wondered aloud if it might not be dangerous.

"Usually, when there's been one try," Clint said, "and I'm not dead, folks tend to leave me alone."

A time or two as they were walking, people would cross the street rather than pass by them.

"Does that bother you?"

"No," he said. "Either they're afraid someone will try again and they don't want to be hit by flying lead, or they're simply afraid. Either way, there's nothing I can do about it."

They stopped in a small saloon for one beer each, and then continued to walk. Eventually, they made their way back to their hotel. As they entered her room, Clint saw there was no telegram on the floor, but then something occurred to him.

"Wait a minute."

He crossed the hall to the room they had taken in his name and opened the door. Sure enough, there was a telegram on the floor.

"They slid it under my door," he said, coming back and closing the door.

"Who's that from?"

"Like I said, Talbot Roper," Clint said.

"What's that one say?"

"He checked out both Hastings and Gentile," he said. "Longtime lawmen, no black marks that he can find. He doubts either one would take up with something like the Knights."

"So that's good news," she said. "It means you can trust both sheriffs."

"It means I may not be able to trust Harriet Willis," he said.

"I already told you to watch out for that bitch," Rita reminded him.

"What is it with you and Harriet?" he asked. "You've got nothing but bad things to say about each other."

"We don't like each other."

"I know that," he said. "It's obvious, but why? Is it a man?"

Rita hesitated, then said, "It was a man, yes. A long time ago."

"And you both still hold a grudge?"

"He was a good man."

"I guess so."

Clint dropped it, which surprised Rita.

"Aren't you even gonna ask me who he chose?" she asked him.

"No."

"Why not?"

"It doesn't matter to me."

"But you're a curious man," she said. "You already told me that."

"About some things."

"So you don't care."

"No."

"Not even a little?"

"No."

She hesitated, then asked, "Do you mind if I tell you anyway?"

"Yes, I do," he said. "If I wanted to know, I would ask."

"All right," she said. "Have it your way."

She sat down on the bed, clasped her hands in front of her.

"I'm tired," she said.

"You should be," he said. "We rode five hours, got into a shoot-out, and then . . . didn't rest. Why don't you go to bed? I'll go over to my own room."

"No," she said. "You don't have to do that. I—I'd like you to stay."

"All right."

They took turns washing in the basin, even though they'd both had baths. He secured the door and window again, just in case, and then they got into bed together. She snuggled up to him, pressing their naked bodies together, and settled her head onto his shoulder.

"Do you mind if we just sleep?" she asked.

"No," he said, "I'm kind of tired myself."

"Good night then."

"Good night, Rita."

After a few moments she said, "Clint?"

"Yes?"

"Thank you for keepin' your promises to me," she said. "That hasn't happened to me very often."

"I'll always keep my promises to you, Rita," he said, then added, "I promise."

She laughed, and drifted off to sleep.

He soon followed.

FIFTY-ONE

An insistent knock woke them the next morning. However, it was not on their door, but on the door to the room across the hall, the one registered to Clint. He got up, pulled on his trousers, grabbed his gun, and went to the door. When he opened it, he saw a small man standing in front of the other door, holding a telegram in one hand.

"That's for me," he said.

The man turned, and it was a boy, about fifteen years old.

"You're Mr. Adams?"

"That's right."

"Eddie—the clerk at the telegraph office—told me to run this over ta ya."

"Thanks."

Clint held out his hand and the boy gave him the telegram.

"He, uh, told me you'd gimme two bits."

"He told you that?"

"Yes, sir."

Clint fished a coin out of his pocket and handed it to the boy.

"Wow! A dollar?"

"Enjoy it."

"Mister?"

"Yes?"

"Are you really the Gunsmith?"

"Yes, son," Clint said, "I'm really the Gunsmith."

"Wow," the boy said again. "A dollar from the Gunsmith. I'm gonna remember this day forever."

He went running off down the hall, and Clint closed the door.

"That was nice of you," Rita said as he sat on the bed. "He will remember this day forever."

Clint unfolded the telegram. It was from Washington, D.C.

"What do you know about Paul Wayne?" Clint asked her. She sat up in bed.

"The Paul Wayne who lives in Utopia?"

"That's the one."

"He's rich, keeps to himself except when he wants to lord it over somebody; then he comes into town and picks somebody out."

"Doesn't like people, right?"

"That's right."

"You think he could be the Grand Master of the Masons?" Clint asked.

"I guess so," she said, "except that he'd have to attend their meetings, and be in a room with a bunch of 'em. I don't think he'd want to do that."

"That's what Charlie said."

"Why are you askin' about Paul Wayne?"

Instead of answering, Clint folded the telegram and put it in his pants pocket.

"We should get dressed and get back," he said. "I want to get to that meeting tonight."

"The Masons' meeting? They won't let you in."

"All the more reason I should get there early." He slapped her on the thigh. "Let's go, if you want to have breakfast first."

"I kinda had somethin' else in mind," she said, reaching for him.

"Forget that," he said, standing up. "You had your chance last night and you wanted to sleep. I'm not easy, you know."

"You're not?"

She tossed the sheet off and arched her back. Her jutting breasts crushed his resolve.

"Okay," he said, slipping off his pants, "so I am, but we'll have to be quick. . . ."

FIFTY-TWO

It had taken them five hours to go from Utopia to Ellerton, but only four coming back. Clint pushed this time, and although he did have to slow occasionally for Lucy to catch up, the little mare proved to be up to the task.

"She's blowin'," Charlie said when Rita handed the mare over to him.

"She had to keep up with that monster," Rita said, indicating Eclipse, who had barely broken a sweat.

"She's a nice one," Charlie said to her.

"Thanks, Charlie."

Clint unsaddled Eclipse, but left it to Charlie to rub him down and feed him. He wanted to get over to the sheriff's office.

He told Rita that when she asked where he was heading.

"I think I'll go home and freshen up," she said, "check in with my boss, and see if I still have a job."

"I'll see you later—and thanks, Rita."

She smiled and said, "What for? Keeping you alive was a selfish decision on my part."

They parted company and went their separate ways.

• • •

When Clint entered the sheriff's office, Gentile looked up at him with no surprise.

"You get your telegrams sent and answered?" he asked.

"I did."

"Checked me out?"

"You came up clean."

"I hope you checked me out with someone trustworthy," the lawman said.

"I did."

"So where do we stand now?" the sheriff asked. "Any word on Bookman or his partner?"

"No, they're still among the missing," Clint said. "As far as where we stand, I've already told you everything. I'm just more at peace with it now."

"What about Harriet?"

"Well, nobody tried to ambush us on the trail," Clint said. "We did have some trouble in Ellerton, but that was from locals."

"Not connected with this at all?"

"Definitely not."

"Okay. What's your next move?"

"Two things," Clint said. "I want to try to meet with more people, and I want to see what I can find out tonight during the Masons' meeting."

"You're gonna sneak in?"

"I'm going to try. Actually, I should've said three things."

"What's the third?"

"I checked out Paul Wayne with Washington," Clint said. "Seems he came here from Philadelphia with a lot of money."

"So."

"Guess what position he held in Philadelphia?"

"I'm really not a good guesser," the lawman said.

Clint tossed his Washington telegram onto the table.

"He was the Grand Master of the local Freemason chapter."

FIFTY-THREE

Gentile read the telegram from Washington and then dropped it on the table. Clint could see by the look on his face that something was wrong.

"What is it?"

"You're lookin' in the wrong direction."

"What do you mean?"

"Just because he was a Grand Master before doesn't mean he is again."

"What do you know that you're not telling me?" Clint asked.

Gentile sat back.

"Okay," he said, "I've gotten to know Wayne since he arrived. He's a bit overbearing around people, which is why he basically stays away from them."

"I've heard that."

"He was a Grand Master, as the telegram says, but he became unhappy with the Masons and he quit. He doesn't want anything to do with them, there or here."

"And you know this how?"

"I . . . go to his house from time to time and play chess with him."

Clint didn't know what surprised him more, that Gentile went up to Wayne's house, or that the lawman played chess.

"So now you're speaking from experience, and not just voicing an opinion."

"It's an opinion based on experience," Gentile said. "He's not the Grand Master of the Knights. Look somewhere else."

Clint frowned. If he was going to trust Gentile, then he was going to have to trust the man's word, as well as his feelings and hunches.

"Okay."

"Okay?" the sheriff asked. "Just like that?"

"I told you, I checked you out with somebody I trust," Clint said. "So if you say he's not our man, he's not our man."

"Well . . . okay then."

"Now," Clint went on, "why don't you give me some idea of where else to look?"

FIFTY-FOUR

Clint left the sheriff to ponder that question and come up with some suggestions. Then he got an idea and went back inside.

"Back so soon?"

"Have you asked Wayne about any of this?"

"Any of . . ."

"What's been going on," Clint said. "The Masons, the Knights, all that."

"Um, he doesn't like to talk about his time with the Masons."

"I think I should go up and talk to him," Clint said. "Will you take me?"

Gentile thought about it and said, "I don't think I will."

"Why not?"

"Didn't you say you'd already met him?"

"Yes, briefly."

"Then go to his house yourself. This way if you say something to offend him, it won't affect my relationship with him."

"Okay," Clint said, "I'll just do that."

• • •

Clint decided to move on his idea immediately, so he went right from the sheriff's office to Paul Wayne's house. It was a two-story brick structure in an area of similar homes. He mounted the front porch and knocked on the front door. When the door opened, he was surprised to find a woman standing there. She was handsome in a stately way, in her forties, with brown hair shot through with gray in an attractive way.

"Can I help you?"

"I'm sorry," he said, "I thought this was—does Paul Wayne live here?"

"Yes, he does," she said, with a friendly smile. "I'm Mrs. Wayne."

Clint didn't know why he was so sure that Wayne lived alone.

"Um, is your husband here?" he asked.

"He will be soon," she said. "He's just gone to the general store to pick up his pipe tobacco. Are you a friend of is?" Her tone sounded hopeful.

"I'm a friend of the sheriff's," he said. "I just wanted to talk to your husband—"

"Well, you're welcome to come in and wait for him, if you like," she said. "I was just making a cup of tea. Would you like one?"

"Tea would be . . . very nice, ma'am, thank you."

"Come in, then," she said, "and don't call me 'ma'am.' My name is Alicia."

"Thank you for your hospitality, Alicia."

She let him in and closed the door.

"This way, please. Truth be told," she said, as he followed her, "I don't have much chance to practice hospitality. My husband does not . . . encourage people to come up here and visit."

"That's too bad," Clint said. "It's a beautiful house."

"Yes, it is," she said, as they entered the living room. "We brought all the furniture with us from Philadelphia."

She almost sighed when she said Philadelphia, and he could tell she missed it.

"I'll be right back with the tea," she said. "Make yourself comfortable."

"Thank you, ma—Alicia."

Clint sat down on a stuffed sofa that seemed to be made of velvet. Did they do that, he wondered? Make furniture out of velvet?

She returned moments later with a tray bearing a teapot and two cups. Also a plate of cookies. She had all the mannerisms of a schoolmarm or a matron, but there was nothing matronly about her.

She set the tray down on the table in front of the sofa and then sat down beside him. She got his tea right, with two sugars, and handed him a cup. He did the polite thing and took a cookie. It was oatmeal.

"I must tell you the truth," she said. "I'm surprised to see you here. Well, I'm surprised to see anyone here. The sheriff is the only person who ever comes up here, and that's to play chess with Paul. So I rarely have anyone to talk to."

"That's a shame," he said. "I'm sure there are a lot of women in town you could make friends with. And I'm certain there are any number of ladies' groups—"

"Oh, no, no," she said. "Paul wouldn't hear of it. You see, we came here to keep to ourselves. We're from Philadelphia, you see, and when we were there my husband was very imp—"

"Alicia!"

She stopped short, tore her eyes away from Clint to look at the man who had just entered the room.

"How many times have I told you, we don't talk to—who are you? What are you doin—hey, wait, I know you."

"Mr. Wayne," Clint said, standing. "It wasn't your wife's fault—"

"You're that fella I met the first day you came to town," he said. "The Gunsmith, right? I didn't know who you were, then."

"My name is Clint Adams." He realized he had never properly introduced himself to Alicia Wayne.

"I was just giving Mr. Adams a cup of tea, dear," she said. "Would you like one?"

"Take your tea to the kitchen, Alicia," Wayne said. "I'm taking Mr. Adams to my study, where I'll give him a real drink." He looked at Clint. "Come on."

"Thank you for the tea and—" he started to say to Alicia, but Wayne cut him off.

"I'll thank you not to talk to her!"

The man didn't wait for a reply. He stalked off to his study and Clint followed because, after all, he had come here to talk to the husband, not the wife. But he felt sorry for the woman. She seemed more a prisoner than a wife.

FIFTY-FIVE

Clint followed Wayne into his study.

"Close the door behind you."

"I'm not sure I'm going to stay."

Wayne was in the act of pouring two glasses of brandy. He stopped, turned his head to look at Clint.

"Close the door . . . please."

Clint hesitated, then closed it.

"Would you accept a drink from me?"

Clint crossed the room and took the drink. Off to the side was a chessboard, with a game already in progress.

"Do you play?" Wayne asked.

"I know the game, but I don't play."

"The town sheriff is remarkably adept at it," Wayne said. "Very surprising."

"Yeah, I found that surprising too."

"You don't approve of the way I speak to my wife," Wayne said.

"I don't approve of speaking to any woman that way."

"What did she tell you, that I won't let her have friends?" he asked. "That I have no friends?"

"Something like that."

"Did she tell you that we moved here because she had a nervous breakdown?"

Clint hesitated, then said, "No."

"I have to keep her away from people," he said. "She can't handle them."

"I've heard that about *you*."

"No," Wayne said, showing Clint his index finger, "I don't like people. There's a difference."

"I see."

There was a desk in the room, but Paul Wayne chose to remain standing.

"So, what brings you to my home, Mr. Adams?"

"The Masons," Clint said. "Or more to the point, the Knights of Misery."

"Yes, I've heard them called that," he said. "What about them?"

"Well, I was going to ask you that question."

"What makes you think I would know anything about them?"

"I understand you were a Mason in Philadelphia. In fact, the Grand Master."

Wayne's face turned to stone.

"Who told you that?" he demanded. "The sheriff? I asked him not—"

"I didn't hear it from the sheriff," Clint said. "I have other sources."

"In town?" He was very tense.

"No," Clint said. "Don't worry. I don't know that anyone in town knows about it."

Wayne's shoulders came down, but his hand shook as he sipped his brandy. Clint took a drink. It tasted all right, but brandy was not a favorite of his.

"Let me ask you this," Clint said. "Was there a problem like this in Philadelphia?"

"You mean a gross distortion of what the Masons are

supposed to be? No, there were no Knights of Masonry in my chapter. I would not allow it."

"Do you think it might have happened since you've been gone?"

"No."

"You know that for a fact?"

"Yes."

"What about here?"

"What about it?"

"You're saying you know nothing about what's going on here with the Masons?"

"Why would I?" Wayne asked, and then it dawned on him. "Wait a minute." He pointed at Clint. "You think I'm the Grand Master. That's it, isn't it?"

"I did suspect that, yes."

"Did?"

"Until somebody vouched for you."

"Really? Someone in this town? I wonder who would do that."

"The sheriff."

Wayne frowned.

"Why? Because we play chess?"

"Apparently," Clint said, "you've said something during your chess games that convinced him."

"That's very odd," Wayne said. "That's very, very odd."

"Why?"

"Well, Mr. Adams," Paul Wayne said, acting very puzzled, "the sheriff and I do not talk during our chess matches."

Now it was Clint's turn to frown.

"Not a word?"

"Sir," Wayne said, "not one blessed word."

FIFTY-SIX

Clint left the Wayne house convinced that Paul Wayne was not involved with the local chapter of the Freemasons. The man may not have treated his wife well, but he was apparently caring for her, looking after her. And so he probably loved her, although he had an odd way of showing it.

But what he'd said about him and Sheriff Gentile playing chess and not speaking to each other was odd. Why would Gentile indicate otherwise? Just when Clint thought he'd gotten to a place where he could completely trust the man, he had to take several steps back. He was back to having no one in town he could trust except Rita.

He was at a loss now where to go. He should probably go to his room and rest up for what he had to do that night, but he wasn't looking forward to seeing Harriet. He sort of wished he had moved out of her hotel before leaving for Ellerton. Then he could have found another one by now.

He decided to bite the bullet and go back to the hotel.

After Clint Adams left, Paul Wayne went to the kitchen, where his wife was sitting at the table, drinking tea and eating a cookie. He walked behind her and put his hands on her shoulders.

"Who was that, dear?" she asked, as if she'd never let Clint Adams into the house.

"No one, dear," he said, rubbing her shoulders, "no one for you to be concerned with."

"Would you like me to make you some tea?"

"Yes," he said, "thank you. Tea would be lovely."

When Clint entered the hotel lobby, he was relieved to see Fred there.

"Hey, Fred."

"Welcome back, Mr. Adams," Fred said. "How was your trip?"

"It was fine, Fred, just fine," Clint said. "You can tell the mayor my trip to Ellerton was very helpful."

"The mayor?" Fred swallowed hard. "Gee, Mr. Adams, I'm just a hotel clerk. I don't get to see the mayor."

"Just remember what I said," Clint replied, "just in case you ever do see him. Okay?"

"Uh, sure, okay, Mr. Adams."

Clint went up to his room and tossed his saddlebags onto the bed. The rifle he propped in a corner. He undid the buckle of his gun belt, removed it, and hung it on the bedpost. Then he sat on the bed, dug all three telegrams out, and read them again.

The fact that Rick had found nothing on Rita, and Talbot Roper had not found anything dirty in the past careers of Sheriff Gentile and Sheriff Hastings, could all, of course, mean nothing. But then his ride to Ellerton would have been a waste of time, and Clint hated to waste his time.

No, he chose to believe all the telegrams. But it didn't mean that Sheriff Gentile might not have gone bad late in his career and joined forces with the Knights of Misery.

As for Rita, he pretty much felt that she had proven herself to him.

And there was still Harriet. Upset with him, she had nevertheless promised not to reveal anything he had told her. Had she kept that promise?

Clint was beat from the ride to Utopia from Ellerton, so he secured the door with a chair, booby-trapped the windowsill, removed his boots, and lay down on the bed for a short nap.

When he woke, it was dark.

FIFTY-SEVEN

He didn't know when the Masons' meeting took place in their "temple." He'd wanted to get there early to try and get inside the building before the members started to arrive.

He washed his face, and realized he was bone-tired. He wanted nothing more than to get back in bed until morning, but that wasn't to be. There'd be time to rest when this was all over.

He left his room, wondering who he could ask about the time of the meeting. When he got downstairs and saw Fred behind the counter, he decided to see what he knew.

"Still here?" he asked.

"Oh, I have to work until late tonight."

"Really? I thought there was a Masons' meeting to-night."

"Oh, I'm not a Mason," Fred said. "I'd like to be, but they haven't accepted me."

"You're kidding," Clint said. "Seems to me you'd be a great Mason."

"You really think so?"

"I'll bet you know everything there is to know about them."

"Oh, I don't—"

"I'll bet you know what time their meetings take place."

"Eight o'clock every Friday evening," he said proudly.

"Well, you'd get my vote . . . if I had one, Fred," Clint said. "Good night."

"Night, sir."

Clint Adams really did seem like a nice man, Fred thought, not at all like someone with a reputation. He wondered why the mayor thought he'd be trouble.

Zack Franklin opened his eyes, realized it was dark. He looked down at his hand, which was still clutching an empty whiskey bottle.

Christ! He sat up quickly in his bed, looked around frantically. Clint Adams was supposed to be dead before the meeting tonight, and he'd gone on a bender. He couldn't remember . . . oh, yeah, he'd taken a whore up here last night. What had happened with Adams? Then he remembered. He'd talked to the liveryman, found out that Adams was probably going to be gone for one day. Out on the trail would have been a good place for an ambush, but he would have had to saddle his horse and then figure out where Adams was going. He wasn't worth shit as a tracker. He'd decided to wait for Adams to get back and take care of him before the meeting.

Now it was dark. He checked his watch and saw that the meeting was going to take place in an hour. Damn! He had one of these blackouts every so often, usually involving a whore and a bottle. He saw a couple of drops of blood on the bedsheet, so he must've had a good time with the whore.

He got out of bed, leaving the empty bottle behind, filled the basin with water, and just put his face in it. He had an hour to find Clint Adams and kill him. This was probably the best way, just call him out and get it over with.

He left the room, wishing he had time to get something to eat—or maybe even a drink.

Clint found the building the Masons were using as a temple with no problem. The lights were on inside, and there were some men milling about in front, including Al Fortune. From across the street, he could see that although the light shone through the windows, they were pretty much blocked so that no one could look in. He decided to work his way to the back to see if he could get in that way.

The Grand Master came over to the mayor and said, "Have you heard from Zack Franklin?"

"No," Calhoun said. "I thought he was reporting to you."

"Where's your man Fortune?"

"He's out front, acting as security."

"Send him out to look for Franklin," the Grand Master said.

"What about security?"

"We have other men with guns, Benjamin," the Master said. "Use them."

The Master turned and walked away. Calhoun went out front and found Fortune.

"Your friend Franklin was supposed to have killed Adams by now," he said urgently.

"He's not my friend."

"Maybe not, but it's your job to find him and find out what the hell happened."

"Yeah, okay," Fortune said. "I'll find him."

"And if you don't," the mayor said, "Adams is yours."

"For the amount we talked about?"

"Whatever," Calhoun said, "for whatever amount you say. Just get it done."

"Whatever you say, Mayor."

FIFTY-EIGHT

Zack Franklin was good at close work as well as with a gun. He had a knife on his belt on the left side. The last time he'd used it was on that Secret Service agent he'd killed in the back room of the temple. For Adams, though, it would have to be a gun.

After he'd left the hotel, he'd passed a saloon and had been unable to resist going in for just one drink—just to wash out his mouth. By the time Al Fortune found him, he was on his third whiskey.

"Man, everybody's lookin' for you," Fortune said.

"Who's everybody?"

"The Grand Master, the mayor—have you killed Adams yet?"

"You see his body lyin' around anywhere?"

"What are ya waitin' for?"

"I just wanna finish this drink."

Fortune could see that Franklin was drunk, and he probably had been for some time.

"Zack, when did you become a drunk?"

"I ain't no drunk," Zack said. "I just have a little

200

problem—I black out once in a while. Took a whore to my room last night and—"

"Zack Franklin?"

Both Franklin and Al Fortune turned toward the voice. It was Sheriff Gentile, standing just inside the batwing doors.

"You're under arrest."

"For what?"

"You've cut up your last whore in this town," Gentile said. "I don't care who you work for."

The sheriff pulled his gun and got the drop on Zack.

"Fortune, step aside," he said.

Al put his hands out and said, "Hey, this has got nothin' to do with me," and backed away.

"Sheriff," Franklin said, "yer makin' a real big mistake here."

"I've made a lot of mistakes lately," Gentile said. "This is one I'm correctin'. I shoulda run you out of town the day you got here. Drop your gun . . . and your knife."

Fortune could see from the look in Franklin's eyes that he was going to go for it. If he took the sheriff, then he'd probably go on to try the Gunsmith. If the sheriff took him, then Clint Adams was Fortune's.

Along with the other patrons in the saloon, Fortune cleared out, made room for the two men to trade lead.

"Don't try it, Franklin," Gentile said. "You're drunk."

"Not too drunk to take you, Sheriff."

Franklin went for his gun. He was fast, but not fast enough to beat an already drawn—and sober—gun. Gentile pulled the trigger once and Franklin crumpled to the floor, dead.

Gentile walked up to the body to check it, kicked the gun away just in case, then turned to look at Fortune.

"What was wrong with him?" he asked. "I had the drop on him."

"I don't know, Sheriff," Fortune said. "I was wondering that myself."

He turned and walked out.

Clint was behind the temple as Fortune left the saloon and Gentile had some men pick up Zack Franklin's body and carry it out. He thought he heard a shot from out of the night, but couldn't be sure.

The windows in the back of the building were also blocked by something, and the back door was locked. Suddenly, Clint wondered what everyone would think or do if he tried to walk in the front door.

It was a wild notion.

Al Fortune walked back to the Masonic temple, saw that members were now filing in. It was not the time to tell Calhoun that Zack Franklin was dead, that he'd drunkenly committed suicide by drawing on a brandished gun. The thing to do now was to find Clint Adams and kill him.

Fortune figured, with all the questions Adams had been asking about the Masons, he was sure to try and get either a look at this meeting or a listen to it. That meant he had to be around the building somewhere.

And just as he was thinking that, Clint Adams came strolling out of the alley next to the building and headed for the front door.

What the hell?

FIFTY-NINE

"Adams!"

Clint turned and saw Al Fortune standing behind him.

"What the hell do you think you're doin'?" Fortune asked.

"I'm going inside."

"They'll never let you in."

"What are *you* doing, Al?"

"I just watched Zack Franklin commit suicide," Fortune said.

"What?"

Fortune explained what Zack Franklin had just done. Clint was more interested, though, in what the sheriff had done. Maybe Gentile had made his first step in taking his town back.

"He was supposed to kill you before this meeting started," Fortune ended.

"Looks like he messed up," Clint said. "Does the task fall to you now?"

"Yep," Fortune said, "and for a lot of money."

Clint turned and faced the man.

"Well, go ahead then," he said. "Try to collect your money."

"You really intendin' to just walk in there and face them all?" Fortune asked.

"Well, I don't know, Al," Clint said. "How many members are there in a town this size?"

Fortune scratched his chin.

"Actually, not as many as everybody thinks."

"How many of them are Knights of Misery?"

Fortune laughed.

"That name always makes me laugh. There are about six Knights, all of whom wear guns inside."

"And the others?"

"Probably fifteen more, usually unarmed."

"That go for the Grand Master?"

"I don't know if he has a gun."

"Six armed men, huh?"

"At least."

"That's not too bad."

"Come on," Fortune said, "even for the Gunsmith, six-to-one odds is too much."

"Maybe."

"Goddamn," Fortune said, "but this might be interestin' to watch."

"I thought you had blood money to collect," Clint said.

"I could kill you inside and still collect," Fortune said. "I think I want to see the looks on their faces when you walk in."

Fortune walked past Clint, shaking his head, and went into the building. He was the last one to enter.

Except for Clint.

SIXTY

The door was unlocked.

Not only did Fortune want to see the faces of the Masons when Clint entered, he had left the door unlocked.

Clint opened it, heard the droning of voices inside. He was in an entry foyer, and ahead of him was a set of double doors that slid open. He decided to just go ahead and do what he had to do. If Fortune was telling the truth, he was not entering a room full of guns.

That was a big if.

When Fortune entered the meeting room, the mayor looked over at him, but the gunman's face was expressionless. In front of the room, the Grand Master sat on a raised dais and was droning on about something that didn't interest Fortune at all. He realized at that point that he was kind of tired of running errands for the Masons through their puppet mayor. Maybe it was time for things to get shaken up a bit.

Clint Adams was the man to do that.

Clint slid the double doors open and stood in the doorway. The size of the room dwarfed the size of the crowd in it. He wasn't sure what the population of Utopia was, but the men present in that room certainly represented a very small percentage of it. Of course, in his time, he had seen entire towns cowed by a gunman or two. That was usually because nobody wanted to stand up to them and be the one who was killed.

The same applied to a lone lawman standing off a lynch mob outside a jailhouse. Those kinds of mobs arose out of anger and emotion, and none of the men in them thought that he might be the one person killed. When it was presented to them—"Do you want to be first?"—they usually backed down.

Clint was banking on the fact that the Masons—and the Knights—were made up mostly of men who did not want to pull the trigger, and did not want the trigger pulled on them.

As the doors slid open, the men in the room turned and looked at him. From a raised dais at the other end of the room, the Grand Master also looked up.

"Well, well," the Grand Master said, "Clint Adams. Welcome to our humble assembly."

SIXTY-ONE

Clint was surprised to find the Grand Master of the Masons masked. He wore a white hood over his head, which went with his white robes.

The room grew quiet. Off to one side, five men with guns came to attention, but the Grand Master waved them off—for now. On the left side of the dais stood Al Fortune, watching with an amused look on his face.

"Your assassin is dead," Clint said.

"You killed Mr. Franklin?" the Master asked.

"No, I didn't have to," Clint explained. "The sheriff did it for me."

"Ah, has our good sheriff suddenly acquired some courage?"

"He has more courage than anyone in this room," Clint said. "More than you, with your face hidden."

"My face is of no consequence," the Grand Master said. "What matters is what we all believe in."

"And you think all these men believe in you?"

"These men believe in the Freemasons," the Master said. "They believe in the Knights of Masonry."

"You mean the Knights of Misery, don't you."

Even in his white robes, Clint could see the man stiffen at the insulting name.

"Mr. Adams, you're a brave man to come walking in here," the Master said, "but also a foolish one. Any one of these men would kill you. All I'd have to do is give the word."

"Then give it," Clint said, looking around the room, of which he had a panoramic view. He could see everyone. "These men know my reputation, right? Don't they, Al?"

"They know you're the Gunsmith all right," Al Fortune said.

"Then they know that I'll kill the first man who produces a gun," Clint said. He looked around the room, catching the eyes of as many men as he could. "Come on, who wants to die first for the Masons?"

The men whose eyes he did catch turned and looked away. He knew he had most of them. The lynch mob mentality. If it's easy, fine, but if it might cost them their lives, they look away.

"I guess you'll have to leave it up to your Knights," Clint said, pointing to the five men with guns against the right wall.

"You men, this is an interloper in our midst," the Grand Master said. "He must be dealt with."

A man stood up, and Clint recognized him from the general store. Not the owner, but a clerk.

"I didn't sign on for this," he said. "I ain't a killer."

"Me either," another man said. "And my neighbors feel that I've turned against them. This isn't what I understood the Freemasons were all about."

"Here's the door, gents," Clint said. "Anyone who feels the same way can leave."

The two men who had spoken up hung their heads and walked past Clint and out of the building.

"Let's put it this way," Clint said. "Show me a gun, stand up for what you believe in, or leave."

A third man stood up.

"I don't believe enough to go up against the Gunsmith, even if I did have a gun."

He left.

Clint couldn't believe it had been this easy. All he had to do was stand up to them? And they would collapse? He wondered how many members had been bullied into joining, and how many really believed in what they were doing.

"Fortune," the Grand Master said, "show these cowards what happens to someone who stands against us."

Suddenly, Clint saw the mayor in the midst of all the men, his face covered with sweat.

"Um, what?" Fortune said.

The Grand Master turned his hooded head to look at Fortune.

"Kill him!" he said, pointing at Clint.

Fortune looked at the Grand Master, then at Clint, then shook his head and said, "I don't think so."

"What?"

"I decided I don't like you, or your group," Fortune said. "You want him dead, do it yourself."

While listening to Fortune, Clint was looking at the young men with the guns, the Knights. They were chomping at the bit. He knew they'd go for their guns the moment the Grand Master told them to.

"Calhoun!" the Grand Master shouted.

"Fortune!" The mayor stood up, and while his voice was meant to be commanding, it came out a squeak.

"Sit down, Mayor!" Fortune shouted. "This will be decided between men."

The mayor looked around, possibly for moral support, and then sat down.

Finally, the Grand Master looked at the gunmen standing against the wall and said, "Knights!"

SIXTY-TWO

The five men went for their guns, and Clint was ready. What he wasn't ready for was to have some help.

From his side of the room, Al Fortune made an instantaneous decision and drew his gun as well.

The Knights of Misery, believing they were five against one and liking the odds, did nothing to take cover at first. They stood straight up, and all five were cleanly outdrawn by both Clint and Fortune.

As the shooting started, the crowd did one of two things. Some of them hit the floor, and the others ran for the door. That meant that some of them were now running between Clint and the Knights.

Clint fired once and a Knight fell, but then there were too many people in his way and he didn't want to hit any of them.

The Knights, however, had no such qualms. They continued to fire at Clint, hitting passing Masons and sending them to the floor.

Fortune, who was standing on the end of the raised dais, had no problem shooting over the heads of the running men. He fired three times and two Knights fell to the floor.

The others, now realizing they were being fired at from two directions, panicked. One of them joined the throng and started for the door. Clint intercepted him and clubbed him to the floor with his gun.

The last of the Knights ran for the dais and the protection of the Grand Master. His leader produced a gun from beneath his robe and shot the man dead, then turned and fired at Fortune before the man could see it coming. The bullet struck him and he spun and then went down.

As suddenly as it started, the shooting stopped. The men who had hit the floor stood up slowly, looking around the room, wide-eyed.

"Get out, all of you," Clint said, "and next time pick your alliances more carefully."

They exchanged glances with one another, and then quickly made for the door.

That left only Clint and the Grand Master standing, both holding guns. Seeing this, the Grand Master hastily tossed his gun away.

"I'm unarmed," he said, holding up his hands.

"I should kill you anyway," Clint said. "You convinced a town full of people that they were in the minority, that the town was full of Masons. Neighbors were afraid to trust neighbors; friends were afraid to trust friends. It's all over now, Grand Master. I was here to make a report to the government about whether or not they should come in and intervene. You killed one of their men, probably right here, and somehow you reached out to Washington to kill the other."

"We have many members across the country," the man said.

"Well, I hope you have some members in prison, because that's where you're going."

"You're not going to kill me?"

"I'm taking you in."

"You're a foolish, foolish man, Mr. Adams," the man said. "I can reach out from prison and have you killed."

"As easily as you had me killed tonight?" Clint asked. "I don't think so."

Clint holstered his weapon. As he did so, he heard footsteps from behind him. He turned and saw Sheriff Gentile run into the room.

"What the—Adams!"

The warning came too late. The Grand Master had produced another gun from beneath his robe and was pointing it at Clint's back. But when the shot came, it was not from that gun, but Al Fortune's. The wounded gunman raised himself up from the floor just in time to shoot the Grand Master, whose robe quickly soaked with blood, and then both men fell to the floor.

SIXTY-THREE

"We really didn't expect you to bust the group up yourself," Dutch said to Clint.

"It just happened that way," Clint said. "As it turned out, it was a much smaller group than anyone thought, and most of the killing was done by one man. For the most part, the others were just confused men looking for a leader in the wrong place."

"And the killer was Zack Franklin."

"Yes."

"And it was the local sheriff who killed him?"

"That's right," Clint said. "Franklin took a whore to his room the night before, and a bottle of whiskey, and he almost killed her. The sheriff was trying to arrest him for that."

"So Franklin killed our man Bookman."

"Yes."

"As for Dan Flood . . . we'll have to see if we can find his killer here in Washington. That won't concern you."

"Thanks," Clint said. "I've had enough of dealing with Masons for one lifetime."

"Jim West was certainly right about you," Dutch said.

"You know how to get the job done. And you didn't have much help?"

"The only person I thought I could trust was Rita O'Doyle, and she was very helpful, but in the end it was Al Fortune."

"The other gunman."

"If not for him, the Grand Master would have shot me in the back."

"And how is Mr. Fortune?"

"He's fine," Clint said. "He's recovering from his wound in Beldon."

"Beldon?"

"Yes," Clint said. "The townspeople changed the name back and put a new mayor in office, a local man named Alex Lincoln."

"And the Grand Master?"

"Dead."

"But were you surprised when you unmasked him?" Dutch asked.

"I was," Clint said.

"Because you recognized him?"

"No," Clint said, "because I didn't. He wasn't anyone I had ever met before, but beyond that . . . he was black."

"A black man was the Grand Master of the Masons?" Dutch asked, surprised.

"Well, no . . . see, his name was Cyrus. He worked as a servant for a man named Patterson, who I had never met the whole time I was there. Like Paul Wayne, Mr. Patterson stayed away from the townspeople. On occasion, he would attend a meeting, but for the most part he used Cyrus as a front—and he had to wear the hood so the members wouldn't see that he was black."

"And they couldn't tell from his voice?"

"Cyrus was very well educated and spoke perfect English," Clint said.

Dutch sat back in his chair.

"So the only question left is, what happened to Mr. Patterson?"

"He's in custody in Beldon on a number of charges," Clint said. "It's pretty clear he'll be going to prison in Virginia."

"Then everything seems to be tied up nicely."

"I suppose so."

"Do you have any regrets?"

"Just one," Clint said. He thought of Harriet Willis and how she had ended up angry at him, but she never did give him away.

"Well, you have the thanks of the Secret Service," Dutch said, extending his hand.

Clint shook the man's hand and said, "Give Jim my best."

"I will," Dutch said, "when he gets back."

Jim West was always off on some job or other for the government.

"Well, when he gets back, give him a message for me."

"Certainly."

"Tell him never to underestimate the lynch mob mentality."

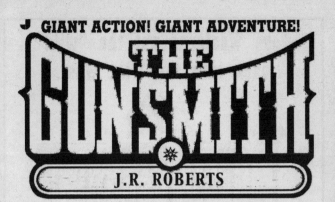

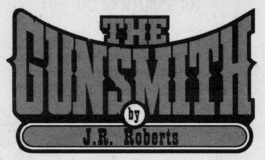

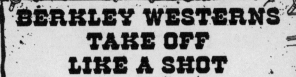

BERKLEY WESTERNS TAKE OFF LIKE A SHOT

LYLE BRANDT

PETER BRANDVOLD

JACK BALLAS

J. LEE BUTTS

JORY SHERMAN

ED GORMAN

MIKE JAMESON

Don't miss the best Westerns from Berkley.